Beware the Bunnyman

Joel Hayes

Fair Weather Clouds—Fond du Lac, WI
ISBN: 979-8-218-24240-4
Library of Congress Control Number: pending
Title: *Beware the Bunnyman*
Author: Joel Hayes
Digital distribution | 2023
Paperback | 2023

This is a work of fiction. The characters, names, incidents, places, and dialogue are products of the author's imagination, and are not to be construed as real.

Dedication

To Dawn, who put the paper in my hand and gave me the opportunity to fulfill my dream. And to Jess, who helped make my dream a reality.

Chapter One

With a synchronized gasp, the congregation of St. James lifted their heads toward the stained glass windows above the altar. A lightning bolt pierced the sky, followed by an immediate percussion of thunder. Unease set over the crowd as the intensity of the storm accelerated. Howling winds could be heard swirling throughout the upper chambers of the old church as the unrelenting gusts found their way into every crease of the wooden roof beams.

A torrential downpour began. Sheets of rain pounded onto the church's aging shingles, but they did their job and held fast as Father Jacob approached the microphone.

Jacob was tall and slender, and age had claimed most of his hair. Elderly now at eighty-two, he was a mere twenty-seven when assigned to St. James in 1946. After being anointed in 1944, Jacob enlisted in the military, serving his time as a missionary. He spent almost two years traveling throughout Europe during the Second World War. After his deployment, late in the summer of 1946, St. James became his permanent home. The church had been constructed in the mid-1800s and is still considered to be a community cornerstone. There have been few changes other than updates to the electricity and plumbing and, thankfully, a new roof.

On the day he opened the heavy oak doors and approached the altar for the first time, Father Jacob felt an immediate connection to the church, which held about 100 people. He had envisioned the wooden pews packed full of smiling faces. Sunlight had poured through the beautifully crafted, stained glass windows, spilling radiant light onto the altar. Jacob bowed, made the Sign of the Cross, and stepped upon it. He knew he had been blessed with his small congregation and had never wanted more.

Jacob's bond with the old church and the town's community reminded him of the Holy Trinity, three entities in one. There was never any doubt that this would be his final resting place. After a brutal bout with pneumonia almost took his life in 1965, Jacob secured his burial plot in the St. James cemetery. "That fever took me closer to death than any Nazi ever did," was his favorite line when telling this anecdote.

For fifty-five years, Jacob had looked out onto his congregation. Some faces had come and gone, but he had preached sermons to many families for three generations, some even four. Today was not the first time Jacob would be speaking over a passing storm, but it would be his last. He was retiring today, on Easter Sunday, on the holiest of days, and unaware that the damage from this storm would continue well past his days on Earth.

Father Jacob took to the microphone with a gentle laugh. Then, mockingly, he raised his hands above his head, looked up, closed his eyes, and spoke, "Oh, thank you, Lord, for giving us all a few extra minutes to make it into Your House this morning."

The priest opened his eyes but kept his head tilted upward. His gaze focused downward onto the crowd, smirking as he continued, "I think I speak for the entire Congregation of St. James when I say, 'Thanks for keeping us dry!'"

Some parishioners laughed, others cheered, and a few yelled, "Amen!" Father Jacob's presence alone eased most anxieties, and his calm, well-aged voice soothed the rest. The church was at capacity today, not only for the Father's retirement but also for Easter Sunday mass. "We," he gestured to himself and the young priest standing slightly behind his right shoulder, "are humbled by your presence today. Thank you for braving this awful storm to come see us."

The young priest smiled and nodded toward the congregation, agreeing with Jacob's words. Father Brian was to relieve Jacob of his position after today's mass. Brian had been assigned to St. James for almost five months and had been doing his best to acquaint himself with his new community and parish members.

St. James was Brian's first congregation to oversee after he had been anointed to the priesthood. He was a young man of only twenty-five. Shorter than Father Jacob by almost a foot, Brian was practically the opposite in appearance. His head was full of dark black hair, and his muscular build was more reminiscent of an athlete's than a priest's. Brian was average-looking, but his personality and smile made him quite attractive. During his short time with the church, he had made an impression of a gentle, kind man, always smiling at the world around him. They were sad to see Father Jacob retire but accepted Father Brian with open arms.

Brian had a way of finding the good in all situations. It was rare for him not to connect with someone immediately. He believed no true evil existed and that love and kindness would always prevail. However, it had not always been this way. Brian had adopted these feelings over countless hours of prayer and self-realization. He now had undying faith in God and humanity. But the path had been rocky, and to this day, Brian had never received proof that God existed. His faith was that of a blind man.

Brian had come from a broken home. Born on Staten Island, he grew up with no siblings or close relatives to bond with. His mother had abandoned him and his father early in Brian's life. He had no memory of her. When he was younger, he recalled seeing pictures of her, but they left no impression on him. Brian's only attachment to his mother was their similar appearance. His father had little formal education and worked a second-shift job as a taxi driver. He struggled to make ends meet and often worked double shifts to support the two. As a result, Brian and his father had a relationship based on duty and respect. Emotional conversations were rare, as work and responsibility were always the main focus.

Brian had never desired a girlfriend. The damage of his mother's abandonment hurt more than he could admit. He was attracted to women but could never pursue a relationship. An invisible wall of fear and resentment stood between him and any girl that caught his eye. He didn't feel like he deserved to be loved by a female and was not willing to take the chance of being rejected again.

Accepting this lifestyle, Brian focused on school and holding down a job. He spent most of his time at one or the other and began working at thirteen to help pay for his living expenses. His father didn't demand this, but Brian felt it was his duty. If Brian had free time, he spent it at the library. The rows and rows of books were more inviting than their tiny, two-bedroom apartment high up on the sixth floor, which was not equipped with an elevator. Brian was conditioned to leave the apartment early in the morning and not return until it was time to eat supper or go to bed. His father always said, "One trip down the stairs; one trip up."

After growing up in daycares and navigating through elementary school, Brian developed an outgoing personality. He presented himself as a good-natured, funny young man even though deep inside, he felt an emptiness and longed for love. While in middle school, his father was diagnosed with pancreatic cancer. The chemo treatments traumatized Brian as he watched his father wither away into a shell of a man.

At the beginning of Brian's freshman year, the only person Brian had ever found solace in passed away. Because he had no other relatives, Brian was placed into foster care. Fortunately, the family that took him in also lived on the Island and had several other teenagers staying with them. One of the young men who lived there, Bishop, ended up being the person responsible for leading Brian to the Church.

Bishop Johnson was two years older than Brian. He had just entered his senior year of high school when

Brian came to live with his foster family. Bishop was initially quiet, but his fun-loving personality emerged quickly. He was well-liked and polite. Bishop had opportunities awaiting him after graduation with an industrial farming company that offered him housing. Brian and Bishop shared a room, and Brian's outward personality quickly broke Bishop's quiet exterior. The two young men soon became fast friends.

The first Sunday that Brian lived at the house, he awoke before everyone else and found himself lost in thought at the kitchen table. His nights were always restless, as he had many recurring dreams of his past. He sat at the window watching the sunrise, thinking of his father's life and how hollow it had been. Now that it was over, Brian couldn't help but think of how meaningless it was. His father's life had been one of constant suffering, and that suffering had now been passed down to Brian tenfold.

Brian's thoughts switched to his mother. She was a stranger and may as well have been nothing more than a figment of his imagination. Brian had no idea if she was even alive, but in his dreams, the woman that represented her was always hiding from him. Brian would search in desperation for her. But, every time Brian found her, she would shriek, and her hair would transform into hissing snakes. Then, she would run from him as fast as she could. Brian had stopped chasing her years ago.

The morning silence was disturbed as Bishop casually entered the room. He wore a navy suit, crimson tie, and dress shoes. "What's happening, Brian? Up earlier than me on a Sunday? Nobody does that around here."

Brian replied quietly, "Yeah, I'm feeling a little homesick, even though it wasn't much of a home. Know what I mean?"

Bishop laughed to himself and sighed, "Damn straight, man. You should have seen some of the places I've called home. Some real shitholes. Some real shitty people, too." He smiled brightly. "This place isn't too bad, though."

Brian couldn't help but agree, even though his opinion was based mainly on Bishop's presence.

Bishop continued, "You know what got me through all that shit, man?"

"No, what?" Brian replied, intrigued.

Bishop turned around and posed in his outfit as if he were a model on a runway.

"Yeah, I was gonna ask about the threads." Brian teased but showed even more interest.

Bishop nearly spoke loud enough to wake the rest of the house. "This is my suit for church!" The level of excitement in Bishop's voice was one that Brian had not yet heard during his short stay at the house.

Brian stood up, a little uneasy with the direction of the conversation. He replied sheepishly, "I wasn't raised in a church, with religion, or anything. I was never even baptized." Brian shrugged. "I hardly saw my dad and had no one else. I grew up in front of the T.V. Once in a while, I would tune into some of those preachers on Sunday morning and watch them sweat as they begged for money. That nonsense was always funny to me."

Bishop was visibly stunned. "I can't believe what I am hearing. Get dressed; I got time. Don't worry about looking as good as me; it ain't gonna happen,"

Bishop smirked, "Just make sure there are no holes in anything."

Brian immediately declined as he waved his hands in front of him. "No way, I do not fit in with that scene."

Bishop was not backing down. "No, I'm serious. You need to come with me. I guarantee you've never been to a place like this one. All who come with an open heart fit in."

Bishop could see Brian's discomfort and tried to ease his reservation. "I promise you; I got your back. All that nonsense on T.V. has no heart or soul, man." He agreed with Brian, "You're right; that stuff is all bullshit. It's all about money to them. That crap you're talking about is more like a cult! Where I'm taking you, it's all about the love."

Looking deep into Brian's eyes, Bishop spoke words of encouragement. "I can tell you are filled with love, waiting to explode. I can tell just by being around you. You are special; you bring comfort and happiness into a room with only your presence. Pleasing people and making them happy feeds your soul. You need to find a way to accept that and let it out. I got just the thing for you, my friend." Bishop pushed Brian toward the direction of their room. "Get going, NOW!"

With much hesitation, Brian finally gave in to Bishop's demands. Shortly after, Brian found himself entering his first house of worship. It was the first time Brian had ever stepped inside a church. The crowd was unfamiliar, and Brian was noticeably uncomfortable as they walked to their seats. Bishop saw his unease. "Don't worry, man; remember, you only need an open heart." Bishop recited a short rhyme. "It's not about your race or the color of your skin; it's about your soul and the love from within." Bishop patted Brian on his shoulder and shook his hand. "Welcome to St. Peter's!"

Brian's unease was immediately swept aside. Everything inside St. Peter's lifted his soul: The energy and the songs. The stories and gospels. The community of people. The beautiful cathedral ceiling and stained glass windows. The foreign smells of the candles and incense. The feeling of belonging overtook him immediately, and the emptiness inside disappeared, replaced with confidence and joy. The warmth and love he felt flowed through the crowd, and Brian spent the entire Sunday at St. Peter's.

Brian had been baptized a few weeks later and had not missed a mass since.

Chapter Two

The sky had appeared ominous all morning. You could feel the electricity building in the air as the thunderclouds approached from the west. In the distance, the storm front could be seen at quarter to ten, but it was slow and powerful. It wasn't until ten after the hour that it hit the town of Ashford, Virginia, a rural community whose population could never quite reach one thousand. As always, the Sunday service was scheduled to begin at 10:00 a.m. sharp.

Father Jacob continued his final morning greeting as the storm slowly rolled by. Thunderstorms had been battering the town for the past eight hours. At Jacob's request, Father Brian snuck away from mass to double-check the doors and windows throughout the church to be sure they were secure. As he climbed the steeple steps, Brian realized he hadn't seen Dave Simmons arrive that morning. Brian thought to himself, "That's right. I was supposed to get Dave's table saw from him. Did I even see Dave this morning?" Brian could not recall seeing Dave, Cindy, or their three children.

Father Brian had spoken to Dave on Wednesday about borrowing his table saw to cut up some old 2X4s in the back of the church parking lot. The absence of the family was odd. Mild concern entered Brian's mind. "Dave's family always attends mass.

Always."

During Brian's few months at St. James, Dave or Cindy had missed a service only if one of the children had been sick. The other parent and healthy children would still attend. The Simmons were pillars of the church, and the children were part of Father Jacob's "Fourth Generation." Brian couldn't pinpoint the source of his unease, but something did not sit well with the young priest.

Brian ensured the remaining upstairs windows were secure. Thankfully, there was no water to be found inside the old church. Brian returned to the service to confirm his suspicion. He scanned the standing-room-only crowd, gazing upon the room of familiar faces, but he had been correct. Even amongst the group who stood at the back of the church, the Simmons family, who usually arrived early to claim a pew in the front section, was nowhere to be seen.

Brian spotted the Simmons' neighbors, Carol and Sam Holt, sitting in one of the back pews. He made a mental note to ask them if they had seen the family this morning. The two families owned property next to each other on Weir Road, one of the older, lesser traveled roads south of Ashford. Their adjacent properties were located about fifteen minutes outside city limits.

Father Jacob's final mass outlasted the storm's intensity by twenty minutes. Jacob presented his last communion to the congregation as the sun shone through the gleaming stained-glass windows. The parishioners felt as if they had witnessed a mortal man calm a raging storm and bring back peace with his words. It was a glorious moment for all in attendance.

After Jacob's final words to his congregation were spoken and the lively standing ovation ceased, the front of the room exited first. Father Brian caught up with the Holts in the back. Sam and Carol were an elderly couple and had lived on Weir Road for 60 years. Carol was helping Sam put on his jacket as Brian approached.

"Sammy, the sun is out now. You certainly won't need this," Carol spoke sternly. "Once you get into the car, you'll start complaining that you're too hot. Just let me carry it for you."

Sam was about to argue when Father Brian cut into their conversation. It was a bit rude, but he felt the situation was urgent. "Good day to both of you," Brian spoke so they could hear him over the exiting crowd. "This may seem odd, but did you see Dave or Cindy at their house this morning?"

"Oh, Hello, Father," Sam replied with a smile as he zipped his jacket up, happy to have Brian interrupt the small argument.

Carol spoke for them. "I'm so sorry, Father, we were in an awful rush this morning; we didn't have much time. We were up late last night with Sammy's family. Well, at least it was late for us old people," Carol giggled. "We must've lost power overnight because our alarm clock didn't go off this morning." She looked at Sam with a smile. "Sammy, honey, what time did you get to bed last night?"

Sam spoke casually. "It was exactly 12:30 a.m. I bet that's the latest I've been up in ten years. When I shut my eyes, the storms hadn't even started." He complained to Brian, "By the time I got up, we had lost power, and the wind had taken down the phone line to the house."

Carol continued. "We woke up with just enough time to get here. Can you imagine us old folks sleeping in like that?" She laughed as she grabbed Sam's arm in a showing of solidarity. "We're headed off to Fishersville now, to my sister's house, for a few days."

"That sounds delightful," Brian replied, pressing a bit more. "Did you happen to notice anything when you drove away?"

Carol grabbed her purse to leave and thought aloud, "From what I could see, there wasn't anything going on at their house, so I assumed they were out the door already. But, as I mentioned, we were running quite late."

The young priest looked at Sam. "Did you see them by any chance?"

Sam shook his head with his eyes closed as if trying to clear his thoughts. "All I remember is her yelling instructions to me, like usual." Then he pressed his memory a bit more. "As I pulled out of the driveway, I didn't notice anything, but we were running late. They were probably on their way to church already. But, wait, they aren't here?" Sam looked puzzled.

Carol spoke next. "We were so late this morning! I was sure we would have to stand through service, but fortunately, the Greens offered us their seats. I just assumed Dave and Cindy were sitting in their usual spots." A worry set over the couple now. "This is unusual. Dave and Cindy are always here. They would never miss Easter service."

Sam spoke as if he was sure. "The power must have gone out at their place, just like ours. They probably overslept like we did."

Carol retorted, "Overslept with three children on Easter Morning, Sam? I don't think so."

Knowing the answer already, Brian asked, "So, you two aren't headed back home?"

Sam shook his head back and forth quickly, "No, Father, we're headed out to Fishersville. Going north."

Carol interjected, "I don't know, Sam. Doesn't this seem strange to you?"

Sam argued, "Carol, we must be at your sister's by 12:30. We're gonna be late already! If we aren't on time, there will be hell to pay, even on Easter."

Brian took charge of the situation, "Please, you two, just be on your way. I'll head up front in a minute and give them a call. I'm sure it's nothing to get too worked up about." He looked at Carol and hugged her. "I'm sorry to make you worry, Carol. Please, look up the number for St. Mary's when you get to your sister's house. I'll be spending the afternoon and evening there. Give me a call if you need some reassurance. Father Jacob and I will be there around 1:00." He spoke his afterthought out loud, "If I can't get Dave or Cindy on the phone, I'll run to the house myself."

Carol exhaled a deep breath of relief. "Thank you so much, Father. I'll look up the number when we get there." She turned to Sam. "O.K., Samson, I guess all we can do now is pray. Let's get going." Carol turned to leave and made her way toward the exit.

Sam shook the Father's hand. "Thanks for

checking on the Simmons. I sure hope everything is alright. He looked to Carol, who was now through the oak doorway. "I'm positive you'll be hearing from us. Carol will make up all kinds of worst-case scenarios by the time we get to Fishersville." Sam looked at Father Brian for a second. Then he closed his eyes and lowered his head, shaking it as if trying to clear his mind again. Finally, Sam looked up and lifted his eyes. "I don't have the time to tell the story right now, Father, but once this is all behind you, ask Father Jacob about the Simmons family history. Only we old timers who were there know the connection, but let's pray there's nothing deeper to this than a power outage or the flu. It's so farfetched to consider, but I know I'll hear all about it from Carol for the next hour." Sam smiled, "I'm sure it's nothing, but it's still a crazy story…some real, local history." Sam nodded to Brian, turned, and left to catch up with Carol.

Easter morning had transformed into a glorious, sunny spring day when the old church doors had been pried open, allowing the dry and spiritually elevated crowd to exit. The birds were chirping while taking baths in pothole puddles left by the storms, and the wet grass appeared greener than when they had entered. The fragrance of lilacs and lilies and the springtime mixture of mud and pollen were detected in the breeze. Parents rushed their children to cars to keep them from getting their dress socks wet or their Easter outfits dirty. Then, everyone was off to an Easter celebration somewhere or another. Unfortunately, the weather report called for further scattered thunderstorms throughout the day. The parking lot emptied quickly as the congregation rushed off to take advantage of the break in-between storms to travel to their destinations.

There was going to be a farewell celebration for Father Jacob the following Thursday, so today's parting words with the congregation were brief. Brian remained at the back of the church as Jacob ushered the assembly out the door. The older priest approached Brian, and they met under the doorway. Jacob saw the stress on Brian's face. "My Son, what on Earth is troubling you?"

Brian shifted uncomfortably on his feet as he asked, "Well, Father, did you notice the Simmons family missing from their spot this morning?"

The old priest closed his eyes, hoping to block out negative thoughts and remain calm. "Yes, I had noticed. He opened his eyes and continued. "Several congregation members were also questioning their absence as I said my goodbyes. Please tell me you do not have bad news for me?"

Brian conceded, "No, I have no idea where they are. I asked the Holts if they had seen them at the house this morning, but neither had. Carol said the storm knocked their power out sometime last night. We all pray the same thing happened, and the family overslept; Frank and Carol overslept themselves. I'm heading up front to call them now."

Father Jacob stroked his chin in deep thought as his deep blue eyes blurred over. A few long seconds passed before he spoke. "Yes, please phone them. I'll lock up and be right there. I do hope it is nothing."

The two priests parted in opposite directions. Brian briskly made his way to the front of the church, bowed toward the altar, motioned the Sign of the

Cross, and headed into the office. The church office had no windows, but the sunlight from the stained glass near the altar made the room bright enough so he could make his way to the desk. Brian switched on the reading light, which dimly lit the desktop. He had to tug at the heavy middle drawer for it to free itself from its frame. Father Jacob had brought the desk with him upon his arrival in 1946. He had come across the relic amongst the ashes and rubble of a fallen church in Poland shortly after the war. It was the only salvageable item in the entire church. At a significant expense for a traveling missionary, Father Jacob shipped the desk back to his parent's house in the States. From there, it made its way to the office at St. James and had rested comfortably in the same spot since. It now officially had become Brian's desk, as Father Jacob had gifted it to him that morning.

Brian quickly removed the St. James Church Directory from the drawer and paged to the "S" section. He leafed through it until he found the Simmons family picture. The family was giving the photographer their best smiles. The priest couldn't help but grin at the image. Dave and his sons wore tan suits, and Cindy and her daughter wore matching blue dresses. Dave and Cindy stood behind their three children: Elizabeth, their eldest; Michael, the middle child; and J.J., the youngest. J.J., short for Joshua James, lay sideways on the floor, resting on his right elbow, with his left knee up in the air. Brian wasn't sure of their ages, but he guessed the couple was probably about ten years older than him, placing them in their mid-30's. He recalled that the kids were in the 7th, 5th, and 2nd grades.

Dave owned the family accounting firm, and Cindy was a secretary at the high school. Middle age had treated them well, and the couple still held on to their youthful appearances. They both had grown up in Ashford and currently resided on Dave's family property, which he had inherited throughout the generations of Simmons men. He was an only child, the last male to carry on the Simmons surname, until his two boys' births. Dave, a handsome man of average height, had a slightly receding hairline and had recently grown a beard to cover up a slight double chin. Cindy now wore glasses when she read and had recently started to dye her hair as gray hairs popped up more often than she liked to admit. Regardless, Cindy was a natural beauty who needed minimal makeup.

The children did not fall far from the genetic tree. Elizabeth, the oldest, was petite for her age. It was evident that she would become a beautiful young woman. She had the natural good looks of her mother but her father's dark hair. Michael, the middle child, looked more like his mother than his father. He had blonde hair and was a very well-put-together, handsome young man. One could almost detect a hint of smugness and vanity in his smile. The youngest, Joshua James, looked more like his father than the other two children. He had brown hair and was cute despite his big smile missing most of its front teeth. Michael and Elizabeth looked about the same height as they sat next to each other on their stools. The family's positioning in the picture showed that J.J. loved to be the center of attention.

Father Brian took the phone off the receiver. He

looked to the bottom of the directory page for the family's phone number. He held the phone between his head and shoulder, collected his thoughts, and wondered, "Had I noticed fear in Sam's and Jacob's eyes?" He took a deep breath and released it. "And what on Earth was Sam talking about? Ask Father Jacob about the Simmons family history?" Brian shook his head in doubt. "I hope this is all being blown out of proportion. After all, this isn't Staten Island, where anything can happen. This is sleepy Ashford, where nothing exciting ever happens." That's why Brian liked living there.

Brian focused on the telephone number in the dim light and dialed it slowly, his hand shaking with adrenaline. The line connected and started to ring. Once, twice, three times. Brian's heart began to pump faster. Four times, onward to ten, he removed the receiver from his ear and stared blankly into the glow of the desk lamp. Awful thoughts snuck into Brian's mind, and he quickly shoved them aside as he brought the receiver back to his ear. The ringing continued to no avail. He promptly hung up the phone to try the number again, assuring himself that he had simply dialed the wrong number. Brian picked up the phone to dial again as Father Jacob rushed into the office.

Jacob's face was flushed from making his rounds in such a hurry. Pleased to find everything secure, he now hoped his fears were about to be erased. But as he entered the dimly lit room, Jacob came upon Father Brian with his arm outstretched, phone in hand, about to set it back on the receiver. By the look of concern on Brian's face, Jacob knew he had already made the call.

"Oh, my Lord Jesus, Brian, you are as white as a ghost!" He pressed, "What is it? Tell me!"

Brian spoke as he shook his head and slowly waved his free hand in front of himself to calm Jacob down. "Nothing to panic over, Father. I just tried their number, but there was no answer." He looked back into the directory at the family's page to their phone number. "I'm about to try it again. I may have dialed the wrong number."

Father Jacob shook his head quickly in agreement. "Yes, do try again, please."

Once again, Brian dialed the number very slowly. He knew he had dialed the correct number this time. He let the Simmons phone ring. Ten...eleven...twelve times. Each man stared straight ahead as the rings began, locked eyes, and looked intently at each other as the ringing continued. It was no use. Brian hung up, turned his body towards Father Jacob, and spoke, "I told Sam and Carol if I couldn't reach the family by phone, I would head out to their place and check on them. Quite honestly, I need to check on them myself. I'm more than a little nervous about all this."

Father Jacob broke in, "Absolutely. Brian. Absolutely. Someone needs to check on them at once."

Brian said, "I'll head over in the station wagon now." He thought for a second. "We are due at St. Mary's in just a little bit… Jacob, why don't you head over in the sedan? There's no need for both of us to go out there. I'll only be an hour or so behind you if I leave now."

Father Brian stood up, about to reach for the station wagon keys on the wall above the desk. Jacob spoke next, his frail, lanky body standing before the doorway. "Brian, I must go with you. I will call St. Mary's and tell them we will be late. They will understand. Too many awful thoughts are running through my head already."

As Jacob reached for the phone, Father Brian gently grasped the old priest's forearm before his hand could reach the receiver. He used the moment to ask about Sam's odd request. "I don't know if this means anything to you, Father, but when I spoke with the Holts, Sam told me to ask you about the Simmons family history." Brian pleaded, "What's going on here? What am I missing? Is any of this connected?"

Father Jacob dropped his arm, slumped his shoulders, and closed his eyes as he lowered his chin to the floor. Jacob shamefully shook his head as if about to say something he wasn't proud to admit. As Jacob lifted his head, his eyes remained closed. He paused for a few seconds, then slowly opened them toward the young priest.

Brian looked deep into Jacob's eyes. They were pooled with fear and flamed with paranoia, yet Father Jacob let out a little laugh to calm himself. "Brian, have you been in Ashford long enough to have heard of the Bunnyman?"

Brian was taken aback in complete disbelief at what he had just heard. He repeated the odd name to Father Jacob to be sure he had heard him correctly. "The Bunnyman?" He questioned again, the disbelief intensified.

"The Bunnyman?"

Chapter Three

Brian had heard of the Bunnyman. A few weeks earlier, during a Sunday school class, a few older kids told him to stay away from the "haunted" Bunnyman Bridge if he went out after dark. They were referring to the small bridge on Highbridge Road built long ago as a railroad overpass. It had been well-maintained and was still in use. Brian and Jacob had driven under the bridge several times, but Jacob had never mentioned the legend.

The children spoke of two incidents in the '70s when rumors of a mysterious figure dressed in an Easter Bunny costume allegedly attacked people with a hatchet. Over time, the entity became known as "The Bunnyman." Rumor has it that his ghost now haunts the Highbridge Road overpass, known to most as Bunnyman Bridge, where he is said to have lived in the dense woods surrounding it.

Although skeptical, Father Brian decided to see if the children's stories contained even an ounce of truth. Coming from a large city, he had never gotten caught up in local legends. Brian was uncomfortable questioning Father Jacob, so he found himself at the public library the following Monday. He wanted to ask the local librarian if she knew anything about the Bunnyman. Brian shook his head just thinking about the ridiculous topic.

Dressed in street clothes, Brian approached Lucy DeVoss, the middle-aged librarian, with a wry smile as if about to ask her something out of the ordinary. "Hey Lucy, How're you?"

Lucy shot Brian a warm smile. She was not a church member, but Brian was a frequent visitor at the library, and they had become friendly. Lucy was in her mid-forties and had been working at the library since moving to Ashford a decade ago. "I'm doing great today, Brian." She read his body language and giggled. "What brings you in today? You were just here Friday. Did something spark your interest over the weekend? You look like you have something on your mind."

Brian replied with a laugh, "You're exactly right. Something did spark my interest, and I hope you can tell me more about it."

Lucy rubbed her hands together in excitement. "Whatcha got for me, Father?"

Brian looked her square in the eyes and whispered in a mocking, overly exaggerated tone, "Tell me, Lucy, what do you know about the Bunnyman?"

Lucy's smile spread wide, and she laughed out loud. "Oh man, Brian. They finally got to you, huh?" She shrugged her shoulders. "I guess it was inevitable."

Brian nodded. "Yeah, the kids cornered me at Sunday school." Then, he questioned her, eyes wide and smiling, "Well, whatcha got?"

Lucy pulled out the closest chair next to a table. "Have a seat, Brian, and I'll be right back. Want some coffee? Black, right?"

Brian nodded in agreement and winked at her as he

removed his jacket. "O.K., be back in five; I gotta run upstairs."

Brian gave her a thumbs-up as she made her way to the stairs. He sat down at the table and began humming absentmindedly. Despite the ridiculousness of the children's stories, Brian found himself intrigued and even a bit excited. "Lucy must have some good dirt on the Bunnyman," he thought. He grinned as he glanced around the small building. It was tiny compared to the libraries back home. But no matter the size, libraries always seemed to have the information you sought, even in a small town like Ashford, even on a stupid subject like the Bunnyman.

Brian smiled to himself as he drew a connection. "Priests and librarians are a lot alike. We both serve people and help guide them to find the answers they seek." He laughed out loud as he thought about the libraries back in New York, the streets he grew up on, and his childhood. Then, he lapsed into a daydream, reliving how lonely he had been before meeting Bishop.

Brian had great respect for his father. Even as a little kid, Brian remembered how lucky he was to have at least one parent and an apartment to call home. Sadly, he had met enough kids in school to know that these things were not guaranteed. Even so, most of the time, Brian found himself alone in the belly of the beast. His dad spent all his time working to stay afloat, but ultimately, he failed. After his dad passed, he had nothing to show for his years of hard work. What assets remained were used to cover his funeral expenses. There was nothing left for Brian to hold on to. Only after meeting Bishop and his introduction to the church was Brian able to find happiness.

Brian felt his life's purpose had begun the Sunday morning Bishop dragged him to his first mass. Before that Sunday, Brian knew nothing about Christianity. He did not immediately connect to the praise and worship of Jesus Christ. But Brian felt elated when he felt the joy and love and saw how faith in God, the Church, and Jesus Christ gave people a sense of purpose and self-worth. This was a feeling that he found intoxicating.

Brian took his vows seriously but had struggled with some of the church's teachings. He had never fooled himself by believing that there was one perfect religion. It seemed that, for the most part, no matter what religion you practiced, you were offered hope that your life would continue after death. Religion gave you comfort that your soul had somewhere to go after you died. Brian believed he had a soul and would be with God someday. He had been taught that if he followed Jesus' word and accepted Him as his savior, God would welcome him into Heaven.

What troubled Brian was the idea of worshiping a mortal man as the actual son of God, even though it was the entire basis of Christianity. During Brian's time at the seminary, he memorized Jesus' words and grew to respect the Man. Brian loved the feeling when he preached Jesus' Gospels, yet, he had not truly felt the Lord's fire or Holy Spirit within himself. Still, Brian followed. He had completely given in to his faith but had never seen or felt any proof of God's existence.

"Father? Hey Brian? Are you in there right now?"

Lucy waved a hot cup of coffee before Brian's face.

Snapping back to reality, Brian focused on Lucy standing before him. She held a steaming mug in each hand and an old manila folder tucked under her right arm.

Brian stood up, took his coffee, and thanked her. He pulled out a chair for her at the table. "Thank you, Brian, such a gentleman. That behavior is why I went out of my way to get this out for you." Lucy smiled warmly as she placed the folder on the table and sat beside him.

Once Brian was seated, Lucy removed the contents of what appeared to be a decades-old folder. "This is everything you'll need to know about the Bunnyman to keep up with the local kids," she whispered, nodding toward the folder.

There was excitement and a hint of childish fear in Brian's voice when he spoke. "Oh man, this has got to be the good stuff."

The evidence inside the aging folder offered proof that the stories of the Bunnyman had been confirmed, to some extent. First were the police reports, two separate incidents. The first occurred during the third week of October, and the second incident transpired the first week of November in 1970. Two verified accounts, two weeks apart. Both incidents occurred within a half mile of the train overpass, and the suspect or suspects were never apprehended. The cases went cold due to a lack of evidence, and no other official incidents had ever been reported and investigated thoroughly. Although many unfounded claims had been reported and studied for several weeks, they had been considered hoaxes.

Then there were the articles from various newspapers. The earliest was dated October 22, 1970; it read, "*Beware the Bunnyman!*" and was reported on by the local gazette, "*The Ashford Tribune.*" Another from the same week, from a publisher in another county, read, "*Bunnyman Seen in Ashford.*" Two articles from the following week announced "*The Rabbit Reappears*" and "*Bunny Reports are Multiplying.*" Brian almost spat out his coffee when he read the outlandish titles. Finally, there were articles from newspapers in both Washington D.C. and Maryland. The final report was dated November 17th, 1970. The Bunnyman seemed to hold the public's attention for about a month and then faded away, only to live on in campfire stories and dark bedrooms. The most interesting of all the folder's contents was a laminated picture of the hatchet used in the first incident.

After Brian had digested the information, Lucy retold the whole story. "O.K., so this is how it goes. The first sighting was on Highbridge Road, a bit down from the train overpass to the west. A local kid had just returned from basic training in the Air Force. He had a few days to spend with his family before being shipped to Vietnam. So, the entire family packed into this guy's house to see him off, including his brothers and sisters, grandparents, aunts and uncles, and cousins. The place was packed to the rafters. While he was home, he proposed to his girlfriend, and she accepted."

Lucy giggled as she continued, "The newly engaged couple were in a romantic mood after such a momentous event and decided to step out to "enjoy some ice cream." The two ended up on Highbridge Road, parked off the pavement concealing themselves in a cornfield entrance." Lucy's voice rose with excitement. "Out of nowhere, the passenger side back window shattered!"

"Along with the glass breaking, the couple heard something land in the backseat. Then, as the kid slammed the car into reverse, they heard screaming and saw a figure lunging toward the vehicle. The kid raced back to his parent's house." Lucy paused and pointed to a picture of a hatchet lying among the scattered papers on the table. "This is what they found in the back seat when they returned home."

Brian nodded, "Impressive information, Lucy, very impressive indeed."

Lucy waved her hands. "Oh no, just wait. This is where it gets really good." She continued, "After the two arrived home, they called the police. Here's the report."

Brian picked up the document and scanned it as Lucy continued. "All the facts the two reported are identical except for one thing. First, the window shatters, and seconds later, a figure emerges from the cornfield and appears in front of the car, lit up by the passenger side headlight. Here is the difference in their accounts. According to the guy, the figure is dressed in all white and is wearing bunny ears or an old Easter Bunny costume. The woman claimed it looked more like an old, crumpled-up Ku Klux Klan hood. They both reported that the approaching figure screamed at them about trespassing on private property, his sacred land, and threatened them with violence in various ways. They didn't stick around long enough to hear details. They backed onto the road and got the hell out of there." Lucy blushed, "Sorry, Father."

Brian shook his head and smirked, "Oh, the hell. No problem. Mondays are my day off." Then, Brian commented, almost as if to himself, "This is unbelievable."

Lucy grabbed the second police report and handed it over to Brian. "This is the second incident, and according to police, the only other sighting of the mythical Bunnyman." Brian's eye scanned the report as Lucy proceeded to tell the second tale. "This one took place in the woods south of the overpass. That section of trees stretches out from the Highbridge Road overpass maybe a half mile before running into a road parallel to it. That would be Foster Road. Do you know where that is?"

Brian replied. "I do; I had dinner with one of the church's families who live out there, the Lorinas." Lucy nodded in acknowledgment that she knew who he was referring to. He continued jokingly, "I know of the road, but don't ask me how to get there."

Lucy laughed. "That's unimportant; the main thing to know is that the two roads run parallel." She continued, "A house was being built in that section of the woods at the time. The Baterman family lives there now. Do you know them?"

Brian shook his head, and Lucy continued, "The driveway to the house now belonging to the Baterman's connects with Foster Road. The backside of their property is the woods that runs north into Bunnyman Bridge and Highbridge Road. I bet the driveway to Baterman's house is at least a quarter mile long, and the house is set back pretty deep in the woods."

Lucy's words came faster. "A week after the first incident, the security guard for the construction company was making his nightly rounds. He was responsible for checking the company's new construction sites. It was after midnight, and he was alone as he drove down the long driveway to the house in the woods. As the security guy drove through the thick trees, his headlights caught sight of the job site. He turned into the driveway, which formed a cul-de-sac. As the security guard reported, everything appeared normal as he made the first turn. Then, suddenly, from behind the house, he spotted a figure wearing Easter Bunny ears and white clothing running in his direction. According to the guard, the figure in the bunny suit climbed onto the house's front steps and began hacking away at the railing with, you guessed it, a hatchet."

Lucy caught her breath and continued. "The security guy stared at this crazed person who was now only about five feet away. He knew he should attempt to stop him, but...." Lucy broke from her story to interject, "Could you handle that, Father? I don't think I could. Imagine coming face to face with something that bizarre and terrifying and being all alone. I know it was his job to protect the property, but who would have ever thought he would come upon something so strange? It gives me the creeps!"

Brian realized he had been holding his breath and exhaled as he pondered Lucy's thoughts.

After pausing for a moment, Lucy finished the story. "Understandably, the security guy froze with fear while the nut job whacked away at the railing. The bunny then turned his attention to the security guy. Running straight toward the van, the lunatic spewed the same lines about trespassing and being on private property. The guard remembered him yelling something to the extent of, "THIS IS SACRED LAND! YOU DO NOT BELONG HERE!" He threatened the security guy's life and anyone else's who dared come there in the future. Finally, the security guy had enough and sped out of the driveway. As he drove off, the crazed man threw his hatchet toward the van. In his report to the police, the security guy said the hatchet somehow missed the vehicle and flew past his driver's side window into the woods."

"When the authorities checked it out early the next morning, there were, no doubt, a few chunks of wood taken out of the railing. They inspected the woods where the security guy claimed the hatchet may have landed. The weapon was never found, but there was evidence of footprints and many broken branches nearby. Someone or something had been tromping around in there."

Lucy concluded, "No more sightings were ever recorded, but by this time, the newspapers had picked up on the story, hence those silly headlines you read. A lot of attention was being drawn to the area. A lot of unwanted attention, I might add. The police patrolled the area heavily for quite some time. For a while, out-of-town traffic flowed through Ashford well past curfew. I guess it was quite a circus. With all the attention, everyone here assumed the Bunnyman skipped town due to the publicity.

Eventually, with no more confirmed sightings, the Bunnyman became a legend, a mythical creature of sorts, around here."

As an afterthought, Lucy mentioned, "With a subject as crazy as this one, you can imagine the volume of prank calls made to the police station. So many false police reports were filed over the next few weeks that the department stayed busy. Still, they were all dismissed with basic investigative skills. It was as if the Bunnyman just disappeared."

Lucy had one more thing to show Brian. "This is a research paper written in 1973 by a college student who grew up in Ashford. In it, she recalls 53 different variations of these two stories. All had circulated throughout the area, and the stories spread out through several counties in the state." Lucy handed him the paper. It was a very professional-looking college essay placed in a page protector. "That's where all the really creepy stories are." She giggled uneasily. "The stories of rabbit mutilation. The stories of the Bunnyman peering in someone's window in the dead of night. The stories of children being murdered and hung out by Bunnyman Bridge. The list goes on. They're all in there if you want to read about it." She smirked, "I like to keep my Bunnyman stories light, so I don't need to read that essay more than once. Anyway, it's all made up, except for what I showed you."

Lucy explained to Brian, "The essay's purpose was to prove how local stories and legends can take on a life of their own and quickly spread through word of mouth. In addition, it demonstrates how stories change so dramatically from one person to another."

Lucy concluded, "This seems to be the case with Ashford's infamous Bunnyman."

Brian handed the folder back to her with the essay still in it. "I think I'll keep my knowledge of the Bunnyman light as well."

Together they laughed and toasted to themselves with their coffee cups.

Chapter Four

Father Jacob confided in the young priest. "Yes, Brian, that's right, the Bunnyman. Isn't it ridiculous to even say that name?" He straightened up and got back on point. "Quickly, Brian, tell me, what have you heard?"

Brian told him what he had learned. "I recently spoke with Lucy at the library about it. She showed me the police reports and news stories. In 1970, there were two confirmed reports of a man in a bunny suit, correct? It was late in the fall; a hatchet shattered a couple's back car window. Also, there was an incident at the Baterman's house on Foster Road when it was being built. There were no suspects, and no one was ever caught. Lucy mentioned the legends and stories, but I know very little of those; we didn't discuss that nonsense. She also mentioned the train overpass because it was close to both assaults."

Father Jacob continued interrogating him, "Is that all you know?"

"Well, yes. Why? Jacob, what's going on here?" Brian pleaded.

Jacob sighed. "I don't have time to go into all the details now. We must get going, but I will tell you this…" Jacob grabbed Brian's shoulders and positioned him so they were face-to-face, looked straight at him, and whispered in a low, sinister voice. "What you learned was true except for one major detail. Brian, they did catch the hatchet-wielding man dressed as the Easter Bunny. They caught him after the second sighting, hiding under the train overpass. Shortly after the sighting, he was taken into custody."

Brian stopped him. "What?" He shook his head in disbelief. "That wasn't mentioned in anything Lucy showed me; she seemed to know what she was talking about."

Father Jacob questioned Brian again, "Did you hear about the second hatchet…from those reports? The one the police found in the woods by the construction site?"

Brian answered quickly, "I was aware of the second hatchet, but the police report stated that after investigating the area, nothing was found."

Father Jacob explained, "The police did indeed find the hatchet that night. Without intending to, the Bunnyman led them right to it. He had stomped around in the dark woods, looking for it himself, before the police conducted their search. They found the discarded hatchet with ease. In the meantime, the Bunnyman fled to the woods behind the house, eventually hiding under the overpass." Jacob continued. "The police brought in the tracking dogs, who quickly sniffed the path through the woods and surrounded the culprit under the overpass.

"Yes, yes...who was it then?" Brian tried to coax the name from the old priest's lips.

"The offender turned out to be Thomas Simmons, Dave's uncle. The third youngest of his father's three brothers."

Brian shook his head in puzzlement. "Why wouldn't the police report this? Are you sure it's true?"

Father Jacob assured him, "This is the truth, my son. I was there."

Brian looked to the floor, unable to face Jacob, ashamed that he had questioned his word. Jacob saw Brian's embarrassment and quickly continued. "Please let me clarify. The Simmons' bloodline runs back to the founding of Ashbury. The Family owned all that land before it had been subdivided into lots."

"Dave and Cindy still have the original Simmons homestead over on Weir Road, but the Simmons family sold off most of the farmland and wooded acreage. To my recollection, Thomas was in his mid-fifties when the first construction started in 1970. He had always struggled with mental health issues, and I was told he was also suffering from the early stages of dementia. At times, Thomas couldn't recall the family land being split up and sold off. That's why he threatened these people. He was out of his mind, thinking the new activity was people trespassing on the family land."

Father Jacob elaborated, "Even before the second incident in the woods, a lot of attention had been given to the first sighting. If you recall, the first incident happened right before Halloween. So naturally, the newspapers ate the story up. The police and town officials were extremely relieved that they had their guy, which would mean the end of the Bunnyman."

The elderly priest shook his head in pity. "But then, you see, Brian, this is where the first of the seven deadly sins, "Pride," enters into the equation. As you know, the Simmons family is rich, powerful, and devout Christians; they have always had power and influence in the town. The family would not allow one of their own to go down as the notorious "Bunnyman." So bribes were paid, donations were made, and on that very night, the police report was rewritten before the public was made aware of the apprehension."

Jacob shook his head in disgust and spoke in anger. "Behind closed doors, the police and officials knew they had their guy, and he was being dealt with properly. He was out of the picture, and they knew the crimes would stop. I know that the Simmons family, whom I call my friends, paid the overtime salaries of the police officers out of their own pockets. They paid to have them patrol the town and surrounding roads to make it appear that there was a constant police presence in the area. They made it appear as if the Bunnyman had not been caught but that he had been scared away. The town had to endure a few more weeks of publicity, but as you learned, things returned to normal quickly."

Confused by this new information, Brian needed clarification on one detail. "He was being dealt with properly? What do you mean by that?"

Father Jacob explained. "Thomas Simmons was taken to the hospital for observation for a few days, then moved to a nursing home afterward by the family. As I told you, they could afford to do this. Thomas was admitted to the Saint Joseph Home over in Greenville County. His hospitalization was never discussed, and the family never spoke of him again. That was thirty years ago and the last I ever heard of Thomas. It was assumed he deteriorated mentally due to dementia and eventually passed on. Thomas was the family's dirty secret." Jacob finished with this memory. "He was a few years older than me. If he were still alive, he would be in his mid-80s. God rest his soul."

Father Brian was puzzled. He tried rationalizing with Jacob. "What would a thirty-year-old incident have anything to do with this situation, even if Thomas was of some relation to Dave?" He looked up at the old priest. "This still doesn't make any sense! Their phone was ringing; they must still have power. The whole family must have a case of food poisoning or perhaps was rushed out of town in an emergency." He paused a second and then spoke with assurance, "I know most of Dave's extended family lives nearby, but not all. I have also talked to Cindy about relatives she has in Maryland. So many things could cause their absence, but I'm pretty sure it's not the fault of the Bunnyman's ghost!"

Father Jacob listened to Brian's words, and they settled him for a moment. "Yes, you are probably right, Brian; you are probably right." Then fear crept once more into his eyes. "But, there is still more to tell."

Jacob grabbed the young priest's arm and pulled Brian towards the door. "We have already wasted enough time here; let us be on our way so we can put this awful mystery to rest." He turned and rushed out of the room, past the altar, and towards the old oak doors. Brian switched off the desk lamp and followed quickly after the old priest, grabbing the keys to the sedan as he passed through the office door and toward the altar.

Father Jacob knelt before his cherished altar and gazed at his savior, Jesus Christ, hanging on his cross. Alone as well. Suffering as he did. The old priest then looked at Brian, who was stepping down from the altar. "I will tell you the rest on the way there, but now, let us pray."

The call to St. Mary's was never made.

Chapter Five

Jacob stepped out onto the top of the church steps as Brian locked the old oak door. The sun shone as they exited the church, but another storm front could be seen, slowly rolling in from the south. Jacob turned his face towards the sky. "Quickly, Brian," he insisted, "Let's get into the car and head to the Simmons' place before that storm rolls in. Maybe it will blow south of here." Jacob shook his head sadly, trying to stay connected to reality. "This weather is surely going to mess up a lot of family get-togethers today."

As the men approached the church parking lot, the sun still owned the day. Although, it was becoming apparent that they would be driving directly into black clouds. Father Jacob led the way. "Let us move quickly, my son. I feel the electricity in the air. Can you smell it?" But before Brian could answer, the dark black clouds along the horizon lit up as one giant flash of pulsating lightning struck. A few long seconds later, the thunder rolled ominous and deep, taking time to holler across the land.

The priests were still only wearing their cassocks, and although long-sleeved, the material was not intended for outdoor use. Brian opened Jacob's passenger door and helped him into a light blue spring jacket lying on the seat. Jacob would need it, no doubt. The young priest then assisted the old priest into the car. Jacob was still in good health for his age, but no matter. His bones were old and brittle, and he moved as an old man would. Brian sat in the driver's seat, buckled up, and placed the keys in the ignition.

Brian paused before turning over the engine and looked at Father Jacob, who was sitting, eyes closed, head tilted upwards, towards the few remaining rays of sunshine. His arms were slightly outstretched, palms up, absorbing the heat and light. Brian saw the old priest smiling, which also made him smile.

Jacob opened his eyes, looked at Brian, and spoke kindly to the young priest, "I love getting into the comfort of a warm car on days like this… when the sun is shining, but it's still chilly and breezy outside." Jacob confided in Brian. "Out of the wind, with that glorious sun shining through all these windows to heat up the interior so comfortably, it's like a warm embrace. It's the same feeling I get when I pray to the Lord and feel his presence. I absolutely love moments like these."

Brian paused momentarily and closed his eyes to take in the warmth alongside his friend. Jumbled images flashed through his mind. His thoughts did not focus on the feeling of the Lord's embrace but that of a child held safely inside his mother's loving arms. He had no memory of his mother or of being held in her arms. Yet, he had always longed for maternal affection. So finally, he had no choice but to admit it and open his heart to her; for the first time. He prayed for her and thanked God that she had given him life.

Brian then switched his thoughts to the Lord and felt something suddenly awaken inside him. It was a heat that penetrated him further than the sun's warmth inside the car, but it did not make him sweat or feel uncomfortable. It instead filled his body with fire. Not a blazing bonfire, but a single solitary candle. One flickering flame, and inside the flame, as it danced, he saw glimpses of himself and the Lord. Brian had never experienced such a feeling, but what Jacob had shared with him brought Brian closer to understanding his own relationship with the Lord. Brian opened his eyes and looked toward the passenger seat. The old priest's face looked upon him as if he had just witnessed a miracle. Amid all the panic and doubt, the priests shared a moment of peace.

Brian started the sedan, slowly driving away from the church, leaving its protective embrace. Both men's gazes were firmly fixed on St. James as it faded from sight. They admired its beauty, and in their private thoughts, they each prayed one final time before they departed.

Heading directly into the storm towards the Simmons' house, Brian recalled driving there before. He knew his way. South on Main Street, straight through town, take a right onto Weir Road immediately after The Pancake Shack's old homemade billboard sign. It was an easy drive, but regardless, it would take fifteen minutes to get there. Maybe even longer now that it was evident they would be driving into the rain. The sky inside of town was filled with solitary clouds, which quickly blocked and unblocked the sun's rays, but the entire sky south of the town's limits was a solid wall of black.

Father Jacob fixed his posture in his seat so that he slightly faced Brian and asked over the rising winds.

"Do I have your attention, Brian?"

Brian looked at him, "Yes, Father, you do, but you might have to share some of it with the storm." He looked back to the front window and placed both hands firmly on the steering wheel. The wind had arrived in a solid blast as it hit the front of the sedan. He pushed his foot onto the accelerator to keep up his speed as the sedan fought against the wind. They were still heading south into a black curtain of clouds. Neither was sure what lay on the other side.

Both priests removed their clerical collars from their cassocks. Father Jacob sighed, "We have the time now, so I will continue with what I started to tell you back in the office."

Brian interjected, "Please do, Father. Please help me make some sense of this."

Father Jacob nodded and spoke, "The Simmons family, as I said, has a long history in this town, and what I told you was true earlier. After Thomas was placed into a home and adequately cared for, there were no further Bunnyman sightings." Sweat now covered Jacob's forehead. He wiped the perspiration from his brow with a handkerchief he had found in the jacket pocket. "This story does not move forward from here, Brian, but backward. Its origins go back to 1947, just a few months after I arrived at St. James. You may not believe this, Brian, but I was accused of committing crimes similar to the ones committed by Thomas Simmons."

A perplexed look covered Brian's face, and in disbelief mumbled, "What?"

Jacob continued, "It was quickly obvious that the accusations were unfounded and came solely from the fact that I was new in town." A frown spread across Jacob's face. "The crimes started soon after I arrived in Ashford. Even though I understood why the accusation had been made, I considered leaving St. James." He shook his head as the painful memories surfaced. "Thankfully, the ordeal only lasted a few days, and I look at it now as if it were a test I needed to pass. My faith was no doubt being pushed to its limit." Jacob swallowed slowly and continued. "It was after the third incident that my name was cleared, but the crimes continued for two weeks afterward.

Jacob took a deep breath and began. "1947 was a great year for America. We had won the war. Husbands, brothers, and sons were returning to their homes. I felt at ease for the first time in years. I think the whole country did as well." Jacob nodded to himself and repeated. "I think the whole country did as well." He furrowed his brow, "But, there were also many funerals to attend during this time. Sadness penetrated its way into every city, every town. If death hadn't knocked at your door, it had at one of your neighbor's doors. That fact seemed unavoidable."

As the two priests approached the outskirts of town, they drove underneath a sky that had become black as night. The storm was upon them. Father Jacob caught his breath. "It wasn't just death that brought misery into communities and homes. Mental illness was also a major problem for many soldiers returning home. Many of these men, shell-shocked or suffering from what we now know as Post Traumatic Stress Disorder, received no medical attention or treatments. The institutions were filled at this time, and beds were given to the men with severe trauma who could no longer care for themselves. Unfortunately, you were returned to the street if you could say your name and recite the ABCs." Jacob leaned in towards Brian and spoke with intensity. "It was one of these disturbed men who we must talk about. He paused for a second. "Brian, what I'm about to tell you is completely true."

"Thomas Simmons was not the first Bunnyman."

Chapter Six

Brian pulled his eyes from the road and gave the old Priest a look of disbelief. The winds were too strong to take his focus off the road for more than a moment. He then turned the sedan's headlights on bright as leaves and springtime debris began to fly toward them.

Father Jacob spoke louder than before. "Yes, Thomas Simmons' actions were a copycat or a continuation, you could say, to earlier crimes. The first Bunnyman was Thomas' younger brother, Jonathon Simmons. He was known as "Johnny Boy" to everyone who knew him. I never met him as he was still overseas, stationed in Okinawa, when I arrived in Ashford." Lightning filled the black sky. Large solitary raindrops began to hit the windshield, one drop at a time, a few seconds apart. "Johnny Boy was a few years younger than me. He was 22 in 1947 when he decided to end his life. He hung himself from the side of the overpass on Highbridge Road."

A booming thunderclap followed the lighting that had filled the sky a few moments earlier. Still focused on the landscape outside the windshield, Brian shuttered and exclaimed, "That's the Bunnyman Bridge! Lucy mentioned legends that had spread throughout the area, something about children being hung from that bridge. A paper was written in 1973 about the legends and unconfirmed sightings of the

Bunnyman." Brian's voice pleaded with Jacob, willing him to say what he needed to hear. "Jacob, please tell me none of these legends have truth behind them!"

Father Jacob reassured Brian. "I have read that paper myself, and from what I can say is that most of those stories are fabrications of the imagination by publicity seekers. People dressed in Easter Bunny costumes that ran around in parks or made up stories of a sighting for the newspapers." Jacob shook his head as he closed his eyes and spoke. "But, some of the stories in that report…some hold truth. Some have been passed on from generation to generation, changing and morphing. I can say, as a matter of fact, some of these stories are about two of Dave's uncles, Thomas and Johnny Boy Simmons. Thomas's actions were minor and weak compared to Johnny Boy's."

The two men arrived at the old restaurant billboard. It had broken free from one of its two side support posts and swung wildly in the wind. "Hold on, Father." There was grave concern in Brian's voice, "This storm is getting worse by the second." He slowed the sedan to almost a stop as he turned right onto Weir Road. They were now heading west well below the speed limit. The wind gusts struck the sedan along the driver's side, and Brian turned the steering wheel slightly to correct the car from the push of the gusting winds. Suddenly, the clouds opened up, and the downpour began. Brian turned the sedan's windshield wipers to the highest speed so that he could see the road.

After the turn onto Weir Road, Father Jacob continued speaking. "I know all this because of my strong friendship with Thomas and Johnny Boy's older brother, Frank Simmons. He was the Chief of Police in Ashford for many years and investigated the reports during Johnny's wave of terror. Frank was unaware the man he was pursuing was his brother until he found him hanging off the Highbridge Road overpass." The old priest made the Sign of the Cross across his chest. "Frank succumbed to a stroke in 94', and I administered his last rites and officiated his funeral. Frank would confide in me throughout the years. I would listen, not only as his priest but as a faithful ally. He told me firsthand what I'm about to repeat to you."

Father Jacob clarified the names of Dave's father and three uncles to Brian. "There were four Simmons brothers whose parents were Robert and Julia, Dave's grandparents. They were raised in the same house that Dave and Cindy live in now. Robert and Julia were in their late 60s when I arrived in town. Unfortunately, they both passed away about ten years after I took over the church." Jacob again made the Sign of the Cross over his chest. "They were my first generation of Simmons at St. James. Robert's great-great-grandfather helped build the structure in the mid-1800s. Altogether there have been six generations of Simmons to worship at St. James. I was blessed enough to preach the gospel to four."

Jacob continued to explain. "The four brothers' names were Franklin, Richard, Thomas, and Jonathon. Frank, my good friend, the sheriff, was the first in line. Next was Dave's father, Richard, who started the accounting firm downtown. He was married to a lovely lady, Katherine, who passed away early in Dave's life. She had just turned 40 when Dave was born. If I remember correctly, Dave was starting elementary school when she passed. Richard passed away about three years ago on vacation in Florida." The priest again made the Sign of the Cross.

"Then there was Thomas, the so-called "Bunnyman" of 1970. Thomas never had any children, nor was he ever married. Instead, he had worked for the Town of Ashford's maintenance crew his entire life. He led an ordinary, quiet life until dementia set in."

"John was the youngest of the Simmons boys. He entered the service right after high school and had been overseas, fighting the war in Japan, for almost two years when he returned to Ashford. He was quite a bit younger than Thomas, who was seven when John was born. That is why John was given the nickname "Johnny Boy." He was always considered the baby of the family."

The priest chuckled. "With all those boys in the house, you would think there was a good chance Robert and Julia would have plenty of grandchildren, but it turned out Dave was their only grandson. They also had two granddaughters, Frank's girls. You must have met them by now, Gina and Penny from our congregation."

"Yes, Father, I know them." Brian confirmed, "I knew they were sisters, but I didn't realize they were Dave's cousins. I know they live together on Cranberry Street." He paused briefly, then asked, "Do Gina or Penny have children? I haven't met any."

"No. Dave's three kids are the only children from their generation. "Gina had been married briefly but divorced after only a year. Penny was married once but could not carry a child to full term. I do remember her having at least one miscarriage. Cancer claimed her husband in the early '90s due to an awful smoking habit."

Brian shook his head in amazement, "The Simmons' blood sure runs deep in Ashford, doesn't it, Father?"

"Yes indeed, too many old friends to mourn at once," Jacob answered, then crumpled his handkerchief into a ball and stuffed it into his pocket. "Here is what I know about those awful weeks during the spring of 1947."

The car was now fully engulfed in the darkness of the storm clouds, blanketing the horizon on all sides. The priests had not escaped its grip, and no end was in sight. The thunderstorm was tracking due north as it slowly doused the town of Ashford and the many miles surrounding it. The prevailing winds had ceased, and the rain clouds slowly crept across the sky, making sure not to leave a single surface dry.

"As I mentioned, Frank Simmons told me that his brother John was presumed to be in Japan. The other three Simmons boys were in their 30's at the time." Jacob smirked. "It does seem ironic that the first crime wasn't even committed in Ashford. Instead, it occurred in downtown Lynchburg at the Five and Dime a month before Easter. The Lynchburg police department received an early morning report that a break-in had occurred. The back door had been kicked open, but oddly the only other damage to the store was a broken mirror, and a small amount of merchandise was taken."

"But, what was taken added to the mystery of it all." Jacob paused as if to sort the facts out in his head. "Rope and a few hatchets were the only items missing. But, here is the strangest part, the intruder had also taken the Easter Bunny costume from the storage room."

Brian's eyebrows raised in a questioning look.

"You know, Brian, the costume that shop owners often wear in the days leading up to Easter. It's quite the draw for families with young children. They can visit with the Easter Bunny while Mom and Dad shop... Anyway, that is all that was taken. Due to the nature of the stolen items, especially the hatchets, all nearby precincts were notified. This is how the nightmare began."

Brian couldn't help but interject to ask a question he figured he already knew the answer to. "I'm assuming Johnny Boy was not in Japan?"

The old priest nodded. "Johnny Boy entered the store, but something had happened to him. Who knows, but somewhere along the way, by the time Johnny reached Ashford, he fully embraced that rabbit costume. It became the Genesis of the legend. Perhaps he put it on, looked into the mirror, and lost his mind. Johnny Boy, the youngest Simmons child, had become the Bunnyman."

"I don't believe that any of what transpired was preplanned. Johnny hadn't dreamt of becoming the Bunnyman. He had never used that name or heard it spoken. Bunnyman was a name made up in whispers by the children of Ashford in the 40s. Many years later, the media latched on to it when Thomas began showing up in a similar costume." Father Jacob uncoupled his handkerchief, wiped his brow, and shoved it back into his pocket. "For whatever reason, for you cannot fully understand the mind of a madman, the remaining days of Johnny's life were spent spreading chaos while wearing that awful costume."

Silence fell upon the vehicle.

Chapter Seven

The dashboard clock read half past noon, but it could have been half past midnight from the priests' perspectives. The dense clouds formed thick shrouds that completely blocked the sunlight. Low-lying fields started to fill with rain as puddles turned into small ponds. The country road seemed to disappear as ditches filled with water and overflowed onto the shoulders. Brian realized that the roads were too dangerous to navigate and slowly brought the sedan to a stop under an overpass. "I think we should wait and let the storm pass," Brian spoke as he parked the car. "I hate wasting time, but I think it's best."

Jacob nodded in agreement and replied, "It is probably for the best, as the story does not get any easier to hear." He continued. "Frank received his first call from a horrified mother two days after the Lynchburg break-in. Obviously upset, she reported that her two elementary-aged sons claimed to have interacted with the Easter Bunny and showed her what appeared to be dead rabbit carcasses left in the backyard. Their explanation would have made more sense had it come from the young boys' imaginations rather than reality. Still, the boys swore they were not making it up."

"When Frank arrived at the scene, he was shocked to see that there were indeed two fully-skinned rabbits lying in the backyard. The family with the young boys lived in the country, and their back property line was a freshly tilled field. To the left of the property lived a neighbor who hadn't been home at the time of the incident. On the right side of the property was an overgrown pasture."

"Two terrified boys explained that they had been playing in the dirt by the edge of the field. They noticed a figure creeping out of the tree line on the far side of the field. As they watched the figure approach, it slowly stumbled over row after row of upturned soil. When the figure had fully come into view, the boys saw, to their amazement, the Easter Bunny. Thinking they had nothing to fear, they let him get closer. They froze in disbelief when they saw his soiled costume and damaged mask. The Easter Bunny approached the pair, looked down at them, and with arms outstretched, presented a skinned rabbit to each child. He held the bloody rabbits just inches from the boys' faces and stood still, waiting until the corpses had been taken from him. The Easter Bunny returned to the tree line, never saying a word. Not knowing what to do, the boys watched him amble away. He was long gone when they raced into the house and dragged their mother out to the backyard. Only the two dead rabbits remained."

"Dead rabbits?" Brian questioned. "Was this supposed to be some kind of sick irony?"

Jacob shrugged and continued, "The order of events that unfolded is difficult to recall; so much time has passed. But the first few are as clear to me now as the day they occurred because these were the crimes I was accused of." The old priest sighed, shook his head, took a deep breath, and continued as

Brian looked upon him with sympathetic eyes.

"The fallout from the earlier incident had just begun. It was dark when Frank arrived at the station to complete the paperwork. As he wrote the report, Frank was convinced the culprit was the same person from the Lynchburg Five and Dime break-in. As he was on the phone, informing the local and state police of the disturbing Easter Bunny sighting, another strange call came into the station. This time Frank's young deputy, Nathan Ford, took the call. Nathan was the only other officer in town and usually worked the night shift."

"The second incident took place on the opposite side of town. Nathan took the call from a frantic man who claimed his wife had fainted and knocked herself out when she saw a peeping Tom, or Easter Bunny, in their front door window. When the ambulance and two police officers arrived, the woman was conscious but in a mild state of shock. The husband had deep cuts on his right hand that would require a trip to the hospital. He led the two officers to a maple tree in the yard." Jacob looked squarely at Brian and asked, "I bet you can guess what was hanging from the maple tree branch."

Brian replied sadly, "It had to be a dead rabbit."

"Yes," Jacob confirmed, "They discovered another rabbit, skinned and hanging by its neck. It appeared to Frank that some of the rope stolen in Lynchburg had been used. The husband gave his statement as he waited for his wife to be attended to by the paramedics. He had gotten home from work, and the couple had begun to make supper. Excited to try a new recipe, the wife remembered that she had tucked the recipe card in her jacket pocket hanging by the front door. A strange feeling came over her as she entered the front hall to retrieve it. She felt as if someone else was in the house or as if she was being watched. Unable to shake the sensation, she called out for her husband, who immediately came to see what was bothering her.

As her husband entered the hallway, she began to apologize for overreacting. As she turned toward her jacket hanging next to the door, her heart dropped to her stomach. Out of the darkness, she saw a giant rabbit head, what appeared to be the Easter Bunny. The figure was directly outside the front door window, staring straight at her. Wordlessly, she reached for her husband's arm, tugged his shirt sleeve, and motioned toward the door. When he saw what she was referring to, he instinctively punched the window with his fist, breaking through two panes of glass. At the same time, his wife, overcome with fear, collapsed onto the floor. The right side of her body and head hit the railing as she fell."

"The man said the person inside the Easter Bunny costume never flinched when his hand came toward him through the window. He claimed they stared at each other for several seconds until he turned to tend to his wife. The ominous figure stood motionless as the man checked his wife's condition. He crouched briefly and found her pulse before standing again. When her husband looked back, no one was at the window. He quickly turned on the outside yard light but saw nothing. As he ran to the phone in the kitchen, he noticed something dangling from one of the maple trees in the backyard. The husband quickly wrapped his bloody hand with a kitchen towel and called the emergency number. After arriving at the hospital, the officers questioned the man's wife, whose story lined up with her husband's."

"By noon the next day, the news of the two incidents had spread like wildfire. Although they were suspicious of the Lynchburg thief, the police had no solid leads. Besides the three-skinned rabbits, no further evidence was obtained from either scene. Complete investigations of both locations were done, but nothing more was found. The second incident happened in a residential area on the opposite side of town from the first. A high alert was put out, and patrols of the area immediately increased. Still, with so much wooded area and so few roads, the police had no choice but to hold their breath, hoping the odd encounters would pass. Although creepy and disturbing, the Easter Bunny imposter had not harmed anyone other than the poor rabbits. At this point, I became involved with the case. Frank confided in me that gossip about the mysterious new priest had begun to spread through Ashford."

Jacob traced the sign of the cross in the window fog with his finger. "The last incident I was to be accused of occurred two days after the peeping bunny. I remember it took place on a Friday because this was the day I fled St. James. A man reported a gruesome discovery to the police. Fresh blood was slowly dripping from his mailbox when they arrived at the Country Lane address. The house, tucked deep in the woods, was hidden from the road where the mailbox had been positioned. The man discovered the bloody scene in the afternoon while attempting to check the mail."

"The guy waited for the police to arrive before opening the mailbox. Frank took it upon himself to pull the handle of the metal door down. Skinned rabbits had been shoved so tightly into the metal box that the instant the door swung downward, they began spilling onto the ground. Half the mailbox's contents lay wet with blood and rot on the earth, while the other half was still pressed firmly into the back of the mailbox in a mass of broken bones and meat.

Jacob's nose cringed as he recalled Frank describing the stench. "Frank and Nathan removed the carcasses from the mailbox and added them to the pile on the ground. Nine more skinned rabbits were logged into the rapidly growing inventory inside the evidence freezer. As before, no further evidence was found. By evening, the news of this newest vandalism had made its way into every home in Ashford. By the early morning hours, calls to investigate my whereabouts could not be ignored. As I said earlier, there was no basis for this gossip. People lived in fear of the unknown, and at that time, I was the only unknown in the small town."

Jacob sighed to himself. "As I said, there was never an investigation opened on me by Frank or the department. Frank advised me to always travel with someone or let my location be known. His intuition led him to believe this wasn't the last they would hear from the demented Easter Bunny. Frank prayed they wouldn't become more violent. It was evident that he was nervous."

"I had said earlier that my faith had been tested at this time, which is no exaggeration." The old priest removed his handkerchief from his pocket once again. He was becoming emotional, and tears began pooling in his eyes. He dabbed at them with the cloth. "I fled to St. Mary's because I had nowhere else to go. I lost myself in prayer and reflected on the misery of war and the unprovoked accusations of crimes I had not committed. I had given my life to the Lord; in return, he had given nothing back except death and misery. So why had he burdened me with these false allegations?" The old priest raised his voice slightly, a tinge of anger in his tone. "I was a man of God, but I felt as if people believed I was the devil!"

Jacob gritted his teeth and grabbed Brian's right shoulder as he spoke. "Unbearable emotions filled my heart. It seemed as if my eyes had been opened wide to the true horrors of humanity. I couldn't shake the feeling that Satan's presence was everywhere, whether on the battlefields in Europe or the streets of any small town in the United States. I wasn't sure if I believed we could be saved. For the first time, I worried that Jesus may have died on that cross in vain."

Lighting struck, followed immediately by a clap of thunder. The few seconds of light illuminated the old priest's face. His look of anger changed to relief as he dropped his hand from Brian's arm. "Brian, my son, God did not disappoint. Salvation came to me in two ways. The first was our congregation. During the week of accusations, I was confident that no one would bother to come to hear my sermon that Sunday. It was my first time celebrating Lent at St. James, and you can understand how important those services were to me."

Brian looked solemnly at Jacob and nodded.

"In my sorrow and grief, I had envisioned the entire town as my tormentors; I felt everyone was against me. But to my unbridled joy, St. James was full that Sunday. My congregation, my flock, had shown up to support me. They made it clear that they had complete faith in me. The Lord had given them the strength to fight back gossip and rumors. I realized it was only a few who accused me, not all. My congregation opened their hearts to me that day. That was the day Jesus showed me grace and mercy, but most of all, love. I could discern how Jesus had been accused of crimes he did not commit, yet paid the ultimate sacrifice." Jacob shook his head, "I felt almost shameful afterward thinking of this. Getting caught up in our injustices is far too easy."

Even though Brian couldn't imagine what Jacob had been through, he felt a tinge of jealousy. He knew Father Jacob's faith was much stronger than his own. Brian longed for some sort of a sign. He needed something or someone to tell him he was not living in vain, ultimately destined to fail, just like his father.

Jacob paused to take a breath. "My other savior was Frank, whose friendship showed me the light. He stood by my side for those few miserable days. He listened to people's fears and suspicions about me but never took them to heart. Instead, he gave me solid advice that could have cost him his job. We prayed together and discussed the town's history and the origin of St. James. He told me of the church's construction and shared stories from his great-grandfather's days. We talked about the nature of man, for we both saw glimpses of Heaven and hell in our callings. We discussed both understanding and forgiveness. It was on Frank's advice that my name was cleared so quickly." A warm smile spread across Jacob's face as he recalled the countless conversations he and Frank had.

As Brian caught a glimpse of Jacob's face, he couldn't help but smile as well.

Chapter Eight

Unfortunately, Jacob's smile was fleeting and faded from his face as he continued. "The next atrocity occurred two days after the mailbox incident. It happened during Sunday morning mass, a time I could easily be accounted for. A trespasser caused significant damage at a farm on Breakneck Road, a tad east of town. The farm is now abandoned, but it was quite the operation back then. It was a fur farm that housed mink, lynx, and rabbits. Because many of those animals were of significant value, the owner went to great lengths to protect them. The farm was only left unmanned when everyone attended church on Sunday. Otherwise, someone always guarded the pens. They even had a night guard to keep predators and thieves away from their precious commodity."

"Before church that Sunday morning, rounds were made, and everything appeared normal. But after returning from church and opening the game barn, the farmer realized he had walked directly into a slaughter. Every cage was mangled, and the barn had been severely vandalized. Terrified animals ran wild, looking for safety. Larger animals had attacked defenseless, smaller ones. Blood and fur had been scattered along the main walkway, and dead animals were strewn on the ground. The poor creatures' necks had been snapped, and some had been partially skinned."

Brian's fingers dug into the steering wheel's leather as he imagined the scene but refrained from interrupting Jacob's story with commentary of disgust.

His voice thick with anguish, Jacob proceeded, "The farmer knew that he had 97 rabbits. Twenty-eight of them could not be accounted for. They did not breed an excessive number of rabbits, as their fur was far less valuable than the other animals on the farm. He couldn't understand why someone would have taken the rabbits over the mink or the lynx. The remaining animals were accounted for and returned to their cages or added to the pile of dead carcasses."

"Frank understood the severity of the situation and had an idea why rabbits had been the target. He figured the weight of the stolen rabbits had to be around 120 pounds. The front gate had been locked and untampered with, so no vehicle could have entered. Frank guessed the suspect had to be carrying the animals and was sure the weight burden would slow him down, which meant he couldn't have gotten far."

"In an attempt to apprehend the suspect, Frank, Nathan, and several men from town blanketed the surrounding area. Soon after their search began, they discovered thirteen dead rabbits inside a burlap sack near the tree line adjacent to the farm's property. As Frank had hoped, the suspect must have been struggling and unloaded what he couldn't carry. Frank tracked the thief's movements up until Cook's Creek. The suspect then used the waterway to disguise his tracks." Jacob explained, "Cook's Creek runs almost three-quarters of the way around Ashford. He must have been using this as his travel route. It was valuable information, but still, the thief disappeared without any further trace."

"The search was called off for the night as darkness set in. The suspect's actions had become increasingly violent, and there was concern that someone would get hurt. Anxieties ran higher than ever. The new information was added to the police wire, and all surrounding counties were again on high alert. But it was becoming clear to Frank this would be Ashford's battle." The old priest took a second to organize his thoughts.

"The next crime occurred within twelve hours of the fur farm massacre." Father Jacob shook his head in complete disgust. "All of these crimes are truly repulsive, but I must say, this one is especially obscene. It has always disturbed me more than the others." His aged mouth formed a frown as he continued. "By Monday morning, more rabbit corpses had been found. This time they were discovered at the elementary school. Children who had arrived early came upon a sight no child should see. As they raced each other to the jungle gym, seven dead rabbits, once again skinned, were found. Only this time, the skin removal had been done at the crime scene. Seven rabbit pelts were found on the steps of the playground's metal slide. Each rabbit was hanging by its neck from one of the monkey bars' rungs. Pools of blood had formed under each carcass."

Father Jacob placed both of his hands over his chest. "For my part, I had taken Frank's advice and was staying at St. Mary's. I now had solid alibis for two of the crimes, so Frank was able to publicly clear my name at a town hall meeting. The focus on me ended quickly; new unknown questions and fears were entering people's minds."

"When would the assailant no longer be satisfied with the mutilation of rabbits?"

Chapter Nine

Brian peered out from the underpass. After its initial rage, the rain slowed significantly. The sky was still black in all directions, but he was relieved it was easier to see now. They still had several more miles to go. Father Jacob turned his body slowly to face forward in the seat. Brian could tell that sharing these stories was taking a toll on the old priest. "Shall we try the roads again, Father?" Brian asked.

"Yes, I want to get to the Simmons soon," Jacob replied.

Brian pulled onto the slick road and pressed on, driving faster than he felt comfortable. He was wholly immersed in Jacob's tale. "Please continue."

"The town plunged into a state of outrage. This was the second incident involving children, and parents wanted answers. Unfortunately, there were none to be had. The state was unwilling to get involved because there had been no physical crime against a human. This made matters even worse. Although no person had been harmed, terror flooded the community. It was as if everyone knew the skinned rabbits were only a taste of what was yet to come.

Neighboring counties sent help to patrol the area. Over the next few days, Frank, Nathan, and the officers went door to door, asking questions and trying to calm fears. They instructed the citizens on precautions they must take until this unhinged individual had been apprehended. The men inspected abandoned properties and unoccupied houses. They walked the banks of Cook's Creek to look for footprints or other clues but always came up empty-handed. There was no sleep to be had for Frank. He required two men be on surveillance at all times and insisted one be him."

"Frank confided in me about his feelings of inadequacy and failure. He was in a state of hopelessness. There were too many questions with no answers. He would seemingly chase a phantom for the next two weeks and consistently remain two steps behind."

"Even with the town on high alert and two police officers on duty, the Easter Bunny phantom continued to wreak havoc. Everyone kept their yard lights on at night, yet the demented individual stayed in the shadows and found places to leave his presence known. Over the next ten days, the remaining eight stolen rabbits, plus two wild ones, appeared throughout the town. There had been ten rabbit hangings, one per day. They were always found skinless, swaying from a tree, and hanging by their neck. There was no pattern to where they showed up. The dead rabbits appeared throughout town or on country roads, wherever the shadows allowed. The phantom continued to elude us all. Finally, the officers were pushed to the brink of exhaustion."

Another round of thunder and lightning struck, and the rain intensified. Brian had not loosened his grip on the wheel and flicked the windshield wipers back up to the highest speed. It suddenly occurred to him that if the rain kept up at this pace, they might not make it to Dave and Cindy's. Panic set in for a moment, but Father Jacob's voice soothed him.

"There were a few sporadic sightings of the Easter Bunny, adding more fear to an already uptight community. He was spotted running across random country roads at night. It was plain to see that this was the work of a madman. The spotters always seemed to tell the same story. While driving after dark, their headlights would catch something in the distance. Out of the shadows, a figure would emerge, make its way to the side of the road, then stop."

"As the drivers approached the figure, it would dart into the middle of the road, stop abruptly, and face the front of the car. It was indeed the figure of the Easter Bunny, grasping a terrified rabbit in each palm with his hands high above his head. His prey was helpless, waiting to be slaughtered. Then the figure would sprint into the darkness before the cars could get close enough to identify the suspect."

Jacob paused and caught his breath. "There were two or three more sightings over the next few nights; only these people turned around before they could completely make out the white apparition. They knew better than to get too close; they had heard the reports. The drivers claimed that the figure never pursued them. It only stood on the side of the road and eerily watched them drive away."

"By this time, the children in town were not speaking of the Easter Bunny, nor were they excited about Easter. They were only focused on "The Bunnyman." This name was invented, amid the havoc, by school children." Jacob took a deep breath and continued as he released it. "A deranged soul planted a seed all those years ago, and his stories grew into myths. Sadly, these myths were based on reality at this time in Ashford's history. As I said, it wasn't until the 70s, during Thomas' turn as the Bunnyman, that the newspapers picked up this name, and it became an urban legend around here. Before that, the name "Bunnyman" was only spoken in hushed tones. There was nothing but fear behind the young voices that said that name."

Jacob proceeded. "The thing about Johnny Boy, the Bunnyman, or whatever you want to call him, he was always just a story, a phantom. As I mentioned, very few people actually saw the Bunnyman. It was only based on hearsay that everyone created an image of what they believed he looked like. They invented hiding spots and tried to imagine what he was thinking. Everything was speculation, of course, and with speculation comes fear. Fear of the unknown. His presence was more ghostly than criminal, a ghost that had decided to haunt the entire town."

"The final sighting of the Bunnyman was the third week after the first incident, which undoubtedly led to his demise. By this time, the locals did very little activity outdoors. No one dared to ride a bike or walk alone. Cars drove with the windows up and doors locked. Instead of playing outside or going to a friend's house, children were kept at home. It was truly a traumatizing time for the townspeople."

"It was a teenage boy who saw him next. He had been hunting on his family's land after school when he came upon the Bunnyman. The boy had purchased a .22 rifle and couldn't wait to try it. He knew the possibility of danger that lurked in the woods, but he couldn't resist heading out alone. His adolescent mind told him that he would be well protected with the rifle. The family's woods covered several acres south and east of their house. The area had been searched early in the investigation but hadn't been checked since."

"The boy did not wander far into the woods as his fear got the best of him. Instead, he sat and waited for a squirrel or rabbit to cross his path. Within a half hour, a brown rabbit emerged, racing from the underbrush a short distance from where the boy sat. He raised his rifle and put the scope to his eye, but something plowed into him before he could pull the trigger. The shock sent him reeling backward. Luckily, he landed facing upward, with his rifle still in his right hand."

Brian had so many questions but did his best to avoid interrupting.

Jacob's words flowed faster now. "The Bunnyman was upon the boy. He loomed over the teenager and grabbed the barrel of his .22. As the Bunnyman tightened his grip on the rifle, the boy managed to fire a shot. Although the gun was aimed at the predator's head, the bullet missed and went through his mask, just below the left ear. Frank confirmed the bullet hole when tagging the evidence in later days."

"After the gun fired, the boy lost his grip on the handle. The Bunnyman had control of the gun and held it by the barrel. The teenager only remembers the gun being raised and coming down upon him as he tried to block the inevitable blow. He was left briefly unconscious, and twilight was upon him when he awoke. His .22 rifle was lying a few feet away, broken in two. The groggy hunter made it home before his parents or siblings. He called the police department, and his statement and search of the family's woods brought new light to the unfolding mystery."

Jacob's words slowed. "First was the sighting itself. The boy had gotten a good look at his attacker. He told Frank of the blackened bunny suit, now beginning to tatter and tear. He recalled the pungent smell of death and decay that filled the air. The memory of the horrid bunny mask staring upon him and the thought of his disobedience brought him to tears. He described how the mask, now deformed yet still in one piece, was mostly flattened and black with stain. Two deformed ears had flapped in the Bunnyman's face, no longer holding any shape. The nose and both eyes had been cut from the mask's face. Though enough of the mask remained, preventing the boy from seeing who was behind it."

"Fortunately, this young man's traumatic experience answered one question. When the police inspected the family's woods, Frank and his deputy discovered where the Bunnyman had been hiding. The Bunnyman had made a small shelter inside a thick section of pine trees. Frank explained that the only way to access the location was to belly crawl along the ground. It was well hidden, and if you were to enter it while occupied, you would be caught face down on the ground, defenseless against an attack. This, no doubt, had been the Bunnyman's home. A small fire pit had been dug but was no longer smoldering. Bones of small animals, mostly still caked with meat, were found scattered on the ground. A makeshift bed made from grass and pine needles was positioned under the thickest branches to protect against the weather."

Jacob confirmed, "The most damning evidence was three pieces of cloth, once white, but now blackened with soil, found on the bed. Two pieces were stitched with large, cartoon-like eyes; the other was a stitching of a rabbit's nose and whiskers. One thing was clear, after the previous day's confrontation, The Bunnyman was on the run."

"Somehow, the Bunnyman still made his nightly visits, leaving behind his skinless calling cards. The terrain was such that one could elude detection for long periods. The police still had no leads but continued to go door to door in town and on every country road. They revisited every house, whether occupied, abandoned, or falling down. "Cover it all and leave no stone uncovered." was Frank's favorite saying. "The old priest laughed to himself. "Just like the rain from these clouds." He shook his head and concluded.

"Once again, the Bunnyman had slipped away."

Chapter Ten

Dave and Cindy's house was only five miles away, but Brian was driving well below the speed limit. Rain pounded on the sedan's roof, and Brian could not see more than two feet in front of him, even with the wipers at their highest speed. He didn't want to stop again, but Brian couldn't determine where the road met the shoulder. The fields and ditches were brimming with standing water. His brain, unable to comprehend their depth, imagined them as vast oceans. The swirling gusts of wind formed small white caps. It took all Brian's concentration to focus on the middle of the pavement, relying on the headlights and instinct to avoid the hostile waters.

Father Jacob could feel the tension in the vehicle and understood Brian's anxieties. He knew that Brian was uncomfortable driving, especially in weather like this. "My Son, you are handling the pressures of the day with great courage. Thank you for your bravery and service to the church and its people. You are an honorable man. The world around us may seem like one vast ocean, but have no fear and continue to have faith in the Lord. He will lead us safely to our port."

Brian took a deep breath as his body reacted to the old priest's words, then released a long sigh that helped calm his fears. Whenever he was around Jacob, Brian could sense the Lord. Jacob was a true man of the cloth and had proven that time and time again. Brian had never met anyone who was so comfortable in their own skin and confident in their faith. Being near Jacob was as close to the Lord as Brian had ever been.

Jacob cleared his throat, interrupting Brian's thoughts. "The last act of vandalism occurred during the overnight hours of Good Friday. The scene was discovered on Saturday morning by Drayton Meyer, the caretaker of the church cemetery. He called me, and I, in turn, alerted the police. Drayton escorted Frank, Nathan, and me to the crime scene."

"Several Simmons family members had already been laid to rest in our cemetery. Drayton was also a good friend of Frank's and warned him that it appeared as if Frank, or the Simmons family, was the target of the crime. Drayton explained that the Simmons family plots had been defaced. When we arrived at the gravesites, we saw for ourselves. It was evident the vandalism had been the work of the Bunnyman."

Jacob shifted uncomfortably in his seat. "Nine family members were laid to rest in the cemetery, and a mutilated rabbit was found on top of each plot. Every corpse was positioned as if lying in the coffin below. The rabbits' heads were arranged about a foot below the headstones; their faces turned to the sky. All were found on their backsides, splayed through the middle of their torsos from their necks to their tails." Jacob grimaced at the memory. "These rabbits had not been skinned but rather mutilated and were surrounded by pools of blood. Their fur was stained red, and the poor creature's internal organs hung out of their bodies and spewed onto the lawn. The slaughter had taken place where each corpse had been butchered and laid to rest."

Brian had slowed to almost a complete stop as he envisioned the scene that Father Jacob was describing. Finally, he could no longer contain himself, and a nagging question escaped his lips. "Why? Why? Why would someone do this? It makes no sense!"

"This was an ungodly act that could not be explained." Jacob reasoned. "I have seen acts of war, atrocious acts done by humans to other humans." He shook his head, trying to explain, "Somehow, in times of war and chaos, one can compartmentalize these acts and claim they are the price of freedom or justice. It doesn't matter what side you're on," Jacob concluded, "but the Bunnyman represented pure and simple insanity…perverse and depraved."

The old priest returned to the story as Brian pushed on the accelerator to move the car forward. There were only a few miles left to travel.

"I finally convinced Frank to get some rest. He agreed to take a few hours off for the first time since the young boys saw the "Easter Bunny" appear from the tree line. Frank needed real sleep, not just the catnaps he had been surviving on. His appearance had become that of a much older man. He was unshaven and black rings hung thick under his bloodshot eyes. Frank's brain was not functioning properly anymore as he began to see things that weren't there. He had difficulty distinguishing reality from his imagination."

"I recall an emotional conversation we had the

night that Frank had finally agreed to rest. As we sat on his front porch steps, he confided in me; Frank told me he was slowly descending into insanity. This was the night, it seemed, that the Bunnyman had beaten him. He said he would work the case for one more day but then needed to take a leave of absence. As of Monday, the State Police would be taking over. They had finally agreed to take control of the investigation because an officer's family had been targeted. As a result, Frank would no longer be able to lead the investigation. He was a noble but broken man whose ego had been bruised and who needed time to escape this nightmare. He graciously admitted his defeat."

The rain slowed enough for Brian to see clearly out of the windshield again. The blackness that had engulfed the sedan now passed. The sky was a mixture of grays as the rain clouds thinned. Jacob accelerated the pace of his story as there was so much yet to tell.

"Easter Sunday was upon us. The day of Jesus' triumphant resurrection into Heaven and Johnny Boy Simmons' disgraced exit from this world. It was the day the small town of Ashford would finally learn the truth." The old priest's words came at a rapid pace. "There had been no overnight sightings of the Bunnyman and no reports of disturbances or vandalism. This was the first morning that no activity had been reported in almost three weeks. It struck Frank as odd, but he was relieved. Looking back, this was the proverbial calm before the storm. Frank had no idea what lay in front of him. He had no way of knowing he was blindly stepping into a hell from which he would never fully recover."

In a hushed tone, Jacob set the scene. "Because it was Frank's last day on the case, he and Nathan decided to cover several miles of land between Foster and Highbridge Road. According to their logs, it had been almost a week since the area had been canvassed. They planned to talk with anyone who answered their doors and ask permission to walk their properties. Frank knew it was one last shot in the dark, but perhaps these routine searches would finally end the Bunnyman."

"After several hours of questions and property searches, the two officers turned onto Cardinal Lane, one of the small side roads that connect Foster and Highbridge Roads. For the most part, Cardinal Lane runs through marshland unsuitable for construction. Dr. Wentworth and his wife, Jill, owned the only house on the road. I'm not sure who lives there now." Jacob grinned as he recalled fond memories of the couple. "Dr. Wentworth started the town's first clinic and even saved my life once. He was a good man and a great doctor."

"Anyway, the Wentworths were retired by this time; both were in their 70s and in good health. They owned two properties. One was in Ashford, where they had migrated from Texas. The other house was in Galveston, where the two had grown up, fallen in love, and married. They were in their late 30s when they bought the land on Cardinal Road. It has always been a beautiful property, as it stood then and now, thirty years later. After the doctor's retirement, the Wentworths spent their winters in Galveston and returned to Ashford each summer. They weren't expected back for another month."

"Nathan had conducted the initial search of the property, and Frank had visited the house a week later. He was the last officer to check on the property. The house and small barn appeared secure on both visits. Frank had also contacted the Wentworths after his visit and assured Jill that things were fine.

The Wentworths had been unaware of the maniac terrorizing Ashford until Frank explained the situation. He told her about the crimes and the investigation taking place. Jill asked if they should return to help keep an eye on things. Although, only part-time residents, the Wentworths felt a strong connection and love for the small town. Frank assured her this wasn't necessary and persuaded her to stay in Texas. Frank promised to recheck the house and get back to her in a few days." Jacob shuddered when he recalled how worse things could have been if the Wentworths had returned.

"So, here Frank was again, inspecting the Wentworth property, searching for a ghost. Frank pulled into their driveway, and everything appeared as it had before. Nathan suggested that he check the house and Frank inspect the barn. Frank agreed, and the two separated."

"Frank made his way to the barn. The overhead and entrance doors had not been tampered with and appeared secure. He checked both windows to find that they were undamaged. Next, Frank looked through one of the windows into the barn and noticed the Wentworth's sedan blanketed under a tarp. Everything inside the garage appeared undisturbed."

"Frank abandoned his barn search and joined

Nathan at the house. He crossed the gravel driveway and walked towards the front of the house. The foundation was constructed from field stone and was windowless. He climbed the patio steps and peered into the kitchen through the front window. Nothing appeared disturbed, and there was no movement from inside the house. No shadows crept, and the air inside looked still. Frank made his way along the right side of the house when suddenly Nathan turned the corner. He approached Frank with a look of puzzlement, fear, and adrenaline. Nathan put his hand out to Frank, shaking, palm forward, fingers facing up, letting him know to stop…letting him know to slow down and keep quiet. Frank acknowledged Nathan as his own adrenaline kicked in. Nathan gestured to Frank to follow him."

"The two crept to the back of the house, where Frank immediately saw why Nathan was concerned."

Chapter Eleven

Father Jacob cut into his tale to elaborate on conversations he had shared with Frank, private until now. "I have heard these stories from Frank's lips more times than I can count. I listened to them as they were taking place and countless times after. Together, and with help from the Lord Almighty, Frank and I worked through the burden of his pain. But, unfortunately, the investigation and its aftermath took a permanent toll on him."

Jacob reminded Brian of one crucial detail. "As I said earlier, the Bunnyman was Ashford's secret during this time. News traveled much slower in those days. This was not a story that went beyond the local newspaper, and there was minimal support from the State police. So Frank felt the intense burden of capturing this phantom, guilty of terrifying his people. He couldn't handle disappointing his town. But it seemed no matter what he did, he was chasing a ghost that was always just out of reach."

Jacob's words stabbed at Brian as he recalled his own dreams. The recurring ones in which his mother always ran away. She, too, was always just out of reach. Brian could relate to Frank more than Jacob realized. The young priest found many similarities between his life and Frank's.

Jacob continued, "Nightmares and depression

plagued Frank his entire life. He confessed the heavy guilt he felt to me. Frank could not get past the thought that he had failed John somehow. It would have been different if he could have gotten to him sooner. So much pain and suffering had occurred under Frank's watch, and he had a tough time processing it. Ultimately, the Bunnyman's reign of terror ended, but Frank had not won. There was no possible way he could. The Bunnyman, the phantom that haunted his dreams, was his brother, his flesh and blood, someone he loved. Eventually, with the passage of time and strength from the Lord, Frank moved forward with this life. He could accept and live with the memories of that awful time."

Brian again felt the connection between Frank Simmons and himself. His phantom mother had never been there but always haunted him. She was a specter of the unknown, an unwanted nightmare forced onto him, but he could not exist without her. When he had joined the church in New York, he had diligently prayed for the nightmares to stop. They hadn't yet, not completely, but now they were just a series of bad dreams. She still would appear, but now he let her run away. He, too, had processed and accepted the pain and misery. He, too, had moved forward. He asked himself if the Lord's hand could have made this possible.

As Brian contemplated these connections, he noticed that, although the rain was steady, the water levels around them were no longer rising. The winds had ceased, and the rain fell into a smooth sea. The raindrops rippled as they hit the surface. "Another sign from the Lord?" Brian wondered.

After his brief interlude, Jacob continued, "Frank and Nathan had noted in their daily logs that a tree limb had fallen onto the cellar doors during the winter months. The limb had caused minor damage to the frame, and the two doors could not be opened until the tree limb was removed. The limb was not exceptionally large or heavy. Still, it had been kept in place for two reasons. One was for the insurance investigation, and the other was so it could be used as a deterrent. It was an easy way to tell if someone had tried to enter the house through the doors."

"After turning the corner of the house, Frank could tell that the tree limb had been removed. It had been dragged several feet into the yard as the ground had notably been disturbed along its path. The two doors were closed, but the deadlock was no longer bolted. Neither officer mentioned the bolt's position in their logs because the tree limb had fallen on top of it and obstructed the view. The officers drew their revolvers, knowing this could be the moment. Intuition took over as they began proper police procedure."

Brian reminded himself to breathe as he waited for the story's climax.

"Frank knelt on the ground and pointed his gun at the cellar entrance. He nodded to Nathan, who swung the door open. No one was there. They stepped over the door frame and descended the cement steps to check the entry door to the basement. It was a windowless, solid wood door, closed and resting loosely on its frame. The doorknob had been destroyed, and a hole remained where the handle and latch had once been. Remnants of the break-in lay scattered on the floor in front of them. With guns drawn, the door was pushed open; flashlights aimed into the darkness.”

“Thankfully, no one jumped out at them from the blackness, and no sounds were heard from within. Frank recalled scanning the basement with their flashlights before entering. There was a low-lying ceiling; both would have to duck down to enter and crouch as they walked. Three doors stood in the cellar. One door was made of solid wood and had a lock, while the other two were made from cheaper wood and had lockless pull handles. Other than the water heater and furnace, the basement stood empty.”

“The two entered the cellar together. Frank tried flicking the light switch, but nothing happened. Nathan walked to the left and approached the pair of cheap wood doors. Frank walked to the right, towards the single door. As he tugged on the lock, he found it was securely in place. Frank recalled cracking a faint smile, his last moment of hope.” Jacob jumped in his seat as a lightning bolt touched down just north of the sedan. The thunder that followed was several seconds behind.

Brian glanced to the north and back through the windshield as the lightning caught his eye. He knew that the end of the story was near.

Jacob reiterated how emotional this had been for Frank. “What took place next changed Frank forever. His faith in humanity was destroyed, and he was forced to believe the unbelievable. As I said, it took him several years to accept the nightmare he was about to enter.”

“Frank lowered his gun. Still hunched over as he

turned, he focused his flashlight on Nathan and the door closest to him. Standing in the shadow of Frank's beam, Nathan aimed his pistol and opened the door. He hadn't waited for Frank to raise his gun again. Behind the door was a closet that contained empty wooden shelving running from floor to ceiling. As Nathan's shoulders dropped in relief, Frank saw the third door swing open and heard it slam against the cellar wall."

"Something emerged from the darkness. A creature sprang from a crouching position off the cellar floor. At that moment, Frank had only seen a blur...a gray mass passing through the ray of his flashlight. From the fruit cellar, out of the darkness, the Bunnyman appeared. He pounced on Nathan, swinging wildly as if skipping stones with his hatchet. Fortunately, his first two hacks were early and did not make contact."

"Frank was still on the other side of the room as he momentarily recoiled in terror. His mind was frozen, and he forgot about his pistol. Nathan shrieked in pain as the Bunnyman's third and fourth swings connected with his torso, slicing through his clothes and skin. He then fell silent, unable to breathe. The first hatchet blow had shattered his right rib cage, and the second penetrated his kidney just below the arm that held his pistol. Nathan's arm fell limp, causing him to inadvertently fire two rounds low into the wall."

"The Bunnyman's fifth and final swing connected with Nathan's right shoulder, slicing deep into his flesh and inserting itself into his humerus. The Bunnyman pulled on the hatchet to backswing, but the blade was dull and would not release Nathan's arm from its grip. Unable to pry the hatchet from

Nathan's broken body, the Bunnyman was forced to leave the weapon behind. Nathan slumped to the ground, blood oozing from his wounds. The moment seared permanently into Frank's mind."

"Finally, Frank overcame his shock, raised his arm, and unloaded the six pistol rounds. He fired the shots at head height, trying to follow the Bunnyman's path. The exposed phantom frantically fled to freedom, now defenseless, racing towards the cellar doors. Five bullets missed their mark. Frank didn't remember his eyes being open when he fired. He figured he had shut them in response to what he had just witnessed, trying to block out the brutality of it all. One shot managed to hit its target. The bullet entered the Bunnyman's back and sliced through his shoulder blade. He dropped to his knees for a second but was able to find the exit."

"Before running off, the Bunnyman stood hunched over at the base of the cellar door, backlit by the red glow of a setting sun. The ray of Frank's flashlight beam struck at the perfect angle and found its way through the mask's two eye holes. Frank looked deep inside the eyes of the Bunnyman but didn't recognize the person he saw. The assailant's eyes were set deep into their sockets, and no light penetrated his pupils; the look of a dead man, awake and moving but not alive. Frank sensed fear in his expression, but his eyes held nothing."

"The Bunnyman rushed up the stairwell, and Frank took off after him, not about to let this assailant escape. Suddenly, Frank froze as he remembered Nathan lying on the cellar floor. A split decision had to be made. Frank knew he had to return to help his partner and could not follow as he watched the Bunnyman dart into the tree line behind the house."

"Frank turned and made his way back to Nathan. Blood pooled around his limp body, and the hatchet was embedded in his upper arm. Frank pulled Nathan to the doorway and up the stairs. Nathan groaned in pain as Frank moved his fractured body. He was alive, but Frank knew Nathan's prognosis was grim and hoped for a miracle."

"Once the men were out of the cellar, Frank removed Nathan's jacket and shirt as carefully as possible. Unable to remove the hatchet from Nathan's arm, Frank cut his sleeve off and worked the remaining clothing over the hatchet. Once the clothing was free, Frank wrapped Nathan's torso and arm and placed him in the passenger seat. Frank picked up the radio after climbing in the driver's seat, but Nathan pulled the cord to the microphone. Mumbling, weak but coherent, he insisted that Frank pursue the Bunnyman and that now was the time to end this. In those moments, Nathan pleaded, begging Frank to send an ambulance to the Wentworths...to leave him and get that bastard!"

Father Jacob spoke as if in a trance, fully consumed in the tale. "There was nothing more Frank could do for Nathan. It was a long shot that he wouldn't bleed out, as his appearance was gaunt, and his lips had turned blue. So, Frank called an ambulance, briefly spoke with the state police, prayed quickly with Nathan, and then left to pursue the attacker."

"Did he survive?" Father Brian needed to know.

Father Jacob did not keep Brian in suspense. "By

God's grace, Nathan survived but paid dearly. His arm had to be amputated below the shoulder as the blow had sliced his arm beyond repair. The blade had caused too much damage but also kept him alive. It was embedded deep enough into his arm that it bled minimally after Frank had wrapped it." Father Jacob explained. "Nathan would have bled to death if Frank had attempted to pull the hatchet out. Instead, Frank had properly tied off Nathan's injuries and saved his life."

Brian shook his head in awe and silently praised the Lord.

"Several of Nathan's ribs were broken, one blow had punctured his right lung, and the doctors could not save one of his kidneys. It was a long, painful process that lasted for years, but he eventually recovered." Father Jacob concluded. "Nathan received a large settlement from the State, considering he could no longer work. Eventually, he moved away to get a fresh start. There were just too many bad memories in Ashford."

Jacob pointed out one detail that he wanted to ensure Brian understood. "You must see that Frank's decision to return for Nathan, instead of pursuing his suspect, saved his partner's life. That is without question. Frank was made a hero for his actions, but unknowingly, he abandoned his brother in the same decision. He felt that if he had known it was John running away from him, he would have taken him into custody. John was injured and would have been easy to overcome. Instead, Frank had let him run, giving John enough time to hang himself.

Frank insisted that he should have been able to

save both Nathan and John. For this, he could never forgive himself."

Chapter Twelve

The Simmons house was now a minute or two away. The steady rain had not picked up over the last few minutes. For the first time, Father Brian noticed the trees on the side of the road. Several limbs had fallen during the storms. Luckily, none had fallen and blocked the road. He was going to lead them safely to the Simmons house after all.

Jacob began to finalize his tale as he knew their trip was almost complete. "Frank watched the Bunnyman enter the tree line in the back of the Wentworth's yard and had mentally marked the spot. After leaving Nathan, Frank ran back into the cellar's darkness. He paused momentarily, apprehensive even though he knew the danger had fled. Frank retrieved Nathan's bloody pistol, which had four rounds remaining. He wiped his partner's blood off the gun, placed it in his holster, and dashed across the yard to the tree line where the Bunnyman had entered."

"Frank found the entrance with ease, even in the dwindling light. He spotted a thick blood trail that led directly into the woods. Frank knew the area well; the only passable terrain in the wet marshland would lead to the rail line that cut diagonally through the area. The train tracks could be followed south to Foster Road or north to Highbridge Road, but east or west would take you into miles of wetlands and impassable terrain. However, if you went to the east far enough, you would eventually run into Ashford. Frank moved quickly but with caution, as he was losing daylight."

"It took Frank seven minutes to jog to the train tracks. The disturbed underbrush and blood trail on the ground were easy indicators of the Bunnyman's path. It was clear he was not trying to cover his tracks. Because it ran through marshland, the rail line was elevated several feet. Frank saw the trail of blood climb the gravel embankment leading north toward Highbridge Road. Now he began to sprint as he had a good view of the terrain and was not afraid of being attacked due to the gravel embankments on both sides. It was clear to him the Bunnyman was on the run and severely injured."

Brian could see Carol and Sam Holt's house in the distance. Above them, the clouds filled with lightning, then a crack of thunder. All at once a downpour was upon them again. Brian slowed the pace of the car one final time. He thanked God there was only another minute to drive.

Father Jacob continued. "The blood trail ended at the Highbridge Road overpass. Frank saw significant blood on the guardrail and even more on the tracks to the bridge's east side. Frank peered over the edge to see if he could follow as the Bunnyman had clearly gone that way."

"The chase ended there. There was no need for Frank to pursue the Bunnyman any longer. Frank was overcome with both shock and relief as he saw the Bunnyman's limp body dangling from the overpass. The culprit had tied a short noose to one of the guard rails and jumped to his death. Long shadows of the Bunnyman's corpse formed on the road as the sun fell below the horizon, bringing closure to weeks of torment."

The sedan slowly passed the Holt's house as the rain continued its assault on the priests. The yard was flooded in several areas, but the couple's blacktop driveway was accessible from the road.

"The Bunnyman chose to end his reign of terror on his own terms. Frank wanted to return to Nathan but remembered the ambulance would most likely have been there by now. He calmed himself and decided the best thing would be to cut the body down as quickly as possible. Frank knew he should leave the crime scene intact but feared a vehicle traveling on Highbridge Road would slam into the remains."

"Frank climbed down from the rail tracks and onto the road. He looked with rage and pity at the figure swinging before him. The feet of the costume rested at Frank's beltline. His neck hung at an odd angle and appeared to have snapped. Frank still couldn't see a face; all he could make out was dark hair on the corpse's head. The dilapidated mask faced upwards, but the phantom's head slumped inside. The black eye holes of the Bunnyman stared forward into the darkness that now engulfed the woods. Once pure white, the rabbit suit was now completely black, matted with filth, and reeked of death. Frank checked for a pulse on one of the wrists. Nothing. The Bunnyman was dead."

"Frank quickly climbed onto the rail line, cut down the body, and pulled the corpse to the side of the road. He had mentioned how light the body was, thinking there was nothing to the guy. Frank laid the body on the ground and, in exhaustion, sat down next to it.

While catching his breath, Frank contemplated pulling off the mask. He wasn't sure he wanted to look upon the face of this monster on his own. He didn't know if he was prepared to see what evil hid behind the rabbit mask. Finally, curiosity got the best of Frank, and he decided to unmask the Bunnyman."

The Simmons' property was now upon the priests. Much of the yard appeared to be a newly formed lake with trees growing out of it. Brian carefully brought the sedan to a stop on the road. The rain was torrential, and he could not see the house. Brian adjusted the windshield wiper speed and unconsciously put on the left blinker to turn into the driveway. Unfortunately, the culvert below the driveway's entrance had been compromised. Brian maneuvered through what looked like a fast-moving river. The house was set back off the road and still undetectable through the sheets of rain.

Father Jacob concluded his story as the sedan idled inside the driveway's entrance. "With the courage that remained in him, Frank undid the two buttons that held the mask in place. He clutched the top of the mask by the ears, pulled it upward in one quick motion, and tossed it to the ground. The face was that of a young man. There was something familiar about his gaunt appearance, but Frank did not recognize him immediately. His first thoughts were that of the victims of the concentration camps in Europe."

"Frank told me that he had seen photographs just beginning to be published in America. Pictures of the horrors during World War II by Hitler's fallen regime. He recalled how the starvation and decay of the bodies made them look almost inhuman; they all, sadly, looked the same. Frank noted that all the prisoners' heads had been shaved, destroying their identities. The Nazis had been draining them of their souls before murdering them or leaving them to die. As Frank had studied those photographs, he noticed that some of the victim's eyes still held light, but in others, there was nothing left." During the war, Jacob had seen this look on too many men too many times.

"The difference with this unmasked man was that he had hair, just an inch or two of black hair. That was how Frank came to identify the body. Once he closed the Bunnyman's eyes, the presence of hair made him appear human. Frank's mind slowly cleared as he stared at the corpse before him, suddenly realizing why he looked familiar. Although Frank had not seen Johnny Boy since he had been deployed, there was no doubt the lifeless body in front of him was indeed his little brother."

Brian looked toward the house through the pouring rain. He slowly drove up the driveway as Father Jacob spoke.

"In this moment of unmasking, Frank had journeyed into a new nightmare. A nightmare that had no logic, no meaning. Perhaps the darkness caused him to mistakenly identify the figure, or maybe he was not in his right mind. Yet his own eyes had identified the lifeless body of the Bunnyman. The reality was that Johnny Boy had been behind the mask the entire time. There was no denying it, but Frank was not ready to accept any of this madness. Frank ran back down the tracks and through the woods with all the strength he had left in him. When he arrived back at the Wentworth's property, Nathan was gone. All that remained was the squad car. The passenger door remained open; Nathan's blood was still fresh, pooled on the seat. Frank called for backup and then, overwhelmed by grief, confusion, and exhaustion, passed out and slipped into darkness."

Brian stopped the sedan in the driveway between the garage and the house. He turned to Jacob and shook his head. "I can't even begin to imagine what Frank was feeling. He had to be devastated."

Jacob nodded sadly, and both men sat silently for a moment, listening to the rain pound on the sedan's roof. Finally, Brian looked through his side window toward the garage and noticed the door was closed. It was entirely surrounded by water, except for the elevated path that led to the entry door. Brian noticed the shrubbery along the path had tiny buds forming on their branches. Along with the destruction, the rains also brought rebirth. He then turned and looked out the passenger-side window toward the house.

The original Simmons house was a three-story American Foursquare built by Dave's ancestors' generations earlier. The large attic space had been finished when Dave's family moved in, and Elizabeth, the oldest child, used it as her bedroom. A covered porch, slightly elevated, ran along the front of the house. An addition had been added to one side, so it no longer appeared as a square. This addition had also been built by Dave's ancestors. The house stood still and dark in front of them.

They could see two sides of the house from their vantage point inside the sedan. No lights were visibly shining from any of the windows. All three levels stared down at them with no life behind their glass.

The windows showed them emptiness on the main floor and in the attic. No curtains or drapes were blocking the view into these rooms. Some windows on the second level had blinds pulled down, but due to the lack of sunlight outside, one could tell nothing was shining from within. All looked to be peaceful and quiet inside.

Jacob turned his head and glanced at Brian, who was already looking in his direction. They made eye contact, and Brian's reaction was self-affirmation and relief. He raised his eyebrows and curled his bottom lip downward as he nodded. Father Jacob's look was more of concern but also of some relief.

Jacob spoke first. "It seems to be quiet, doesn't it? They must have been called out of town for something. I hope it was nothing too serious." Jacob paused momentarily, still trying to shake the nagging alarm he felt. "I just don't know. This rain makes it so hard to think." Finally, he concluded, "We will wait here until the rain slows down; then, we can check on the house. Please, Brian, I need the peace of mind." He chuckled to himself. "All this talk of the past has made me overanxious. The wait will also give me a few minutes to finish what I wanted to tell you."

Father Brian answered without hesitation. "Absolutely, my friend; once the rain slows, I'll run over to the garage and make sure the car is gone. I can check the house, too, just to be positive."

Jacob bowed his head and grabbed Brian's hand. "Thank you, my son. I am sure we will be on our way to St. Mary's in no time." He offered Brian a wide, closed-mouth smile before his face turned somber. He straightened his posture and placed his hands in his lap.

"Now, let me finish walking you through Frank's nightmare." Jacob sighed and continued. "Sirens of the incoming backup squads awoke him. In a daze, he led the State Troopers and an ambulance to John's body. Even though he was most likely in shock, he helped throughout the night with the investigation. He could never fully recall what happened the rest of that night. At some point in the early morning, the Simmons family was informed about Johnny Boy's passing. As you can imagine, the news was received with shock and disbelief."

Jacob recalled one final detail. "Frank helped transport John's body to the coroner's office and removed his clothes. The Easter Bunny mask and suit were tagged and put into an evidence locker. Frank spoke of the relief he had felt when the lid of that locker was closed. The phantom had finally been caught and could no longer escape. The Bunnyman was dead, and now Frank could properly mourn his brother. But, unfortunately, the bunny mask made one more appearance in Frank's life that haunted him until his final days on Earth."

"Many years later, on the night of Thomas's capture, the surviving Simmons brothers were called to the police station. Frank was not involved in Thomas's arrest or pursuit and had been semi-retired from the police force by this time. When Frank and Richard arrived at the station, they found Thomas dressed in all white. Frank fell to his knees when the arresting officer pulled out Johnny Boy's Easter Bunny mask from an evidence bag. All the emotion Frank had spent years suppressing came flooding back as he stared at the mask, still stained and covered in dirt and filth. Thomas was found wearing it when he was captured."

"The investigation revealed how Thomas easily retrieved the mask from the police station without being detected. I told you earlier that Thomas worked for the Town of Ashford; therefore, he had access to the town's municipal buildings. He obtained the correct keys for the evidence room and locker when the station was empty. Thomas figured no one would ever miss the mask of a deceased animal murderer who took his own life. It was a perfect crime."

Brian sat in shocked silence. It took him several moments to sort through his thoughts. Finally, he spoke. "Father, how did Johnny Boy return home from the war without anyone being notified?"

Jacob shook his head. "It was a mistake made at the post office that kept John's arrival back to the U.S. a secret. An official letter from the United States Army had been sent to Robert and Julia's house informing them of John's honorable discharge. It also told of John's expected arrival date back home to Virginia. He was to be supplied with the appropriate paperwork needed to get him back safely to Ashford."

"The letter explained John's mental state and the reason for his discharge. He had been diagnosed with shell shock after enduring more than he could process during his time overseas. John had witnessed horrifying visions of death as bombs exploded only feet away from him, incinerating members of his brigade. He had to stand by helplessly as bombs blew women and children into thousands of pieces before his eyes. John watched as burning bodies ran out of bombed-out buildings, flailing in pain until they dropped. Hell on Earth was the only way to describe what John had endured; absolute horror. Unfortunately, the letter never arrived at the Simmons' home. They were not aware of their son's return and the awful mental state that he was in."

Father Jacob explained. "The government traced the letter to the Lynchburg Post Office and located it easily. It had simply been overlooked. The postmaster had momentarily put the letter into a basket of returned mail and forgot about it."

"As for Frank, he suffered a shell shock all his own. But, as I mentioned earlier, he eventually overcame most of this nightmare. Still, one thing could never be erased from his memory; the emptiness in Johnny Boy's eyes as Frank looked into them before John escaped the Wentworth's cellar."

The rain was steadily slowing now.

"The two of us spoke on this subject many times. We talked of the mind and soul. Frank saw nothing behind Johnny's eyes; they were just as empty as the windows in that house." Jacob pointed towards the Simmons' house, up to the attic window, and then turned forward again. "How would John be saved if he wasn't aware of his actions? Frank said he knew John's soul was already gone when he looked into his brother's eyes in the Wentworth's basement. He may not have known that it was his brother he was looking at, but he knew whoever it was, was gone. Gone from reality and gone from the grace of God."

"Frank and I had many discussions over the years about whether or not John's soul could be saved… Frank felt there still had to be a soul that deserved forgiveness behind those eyes, but where? How could anyone ever know what was happening inside John's mind by then? Nothing he did had made sense. His actions were complete insanity...craziness. This man had returned home from bravely serving our country and had been forgotten...misplaced, I guess you could say. He had never hurt anyone until he lost his mind."

"No one deserves to experience what Nathan or any of John's other victims experienced; that goes without saying, but perhaps Jonathan was also a victim. Could his actions have been the pure survival instinct of a living being, one of the insane war casualties? It's impossible to know. Was Jonathan, the man, the son, the brother, in there anymore? Frank's conclusion was, "No."

"Frank had wondered that if John was no longer behind those eyes, mentally gone, how could his soul be saved from the sins he had committed? Does a man need to be consciously present to know of his sins to be considered a sinner? Consciously present when he commits these sins to be a sinner? Consciously present to be forgiven for them? Where was his soul, and could it be saved?" The old priest looked down to his lap and opened his hands upward, palms towards the roof. "Frank wasn't convinced that John could be saved." He smiled, looked towards Brian, and shook his head in pity, placing his still-open hands onto his chest. "I, though, made him see differently."

Brian listened intently, awaiting perspective from one of the wisest people he had ever met. But, unfortunately, what he saw over Father Jacob's shoulder erased all rational thoughts from Brian's mind.

There would be no more storytelling or words of wisdom on this day.

Chapter Thirteen

B rian's eyes locked onto something making its way through standing water on the far side of the house. Whatever it was, it appeared to be crawling through the backyard. "What on Earth is that?" Brian gasped as he peered out of the blurred window.

Father Jacob turned his head to match Brian's stare. They peered through the window momentarily, stunned to see a hand extend from the figure and reach toward them. Both men stared in disbelief and horror as the figure came into focus.

Jacob turned to Brian, who had already opened his door. "Brian," Father Jacob yelled as he exited the sedan, "I'm right behind you! Run!"

Brian could not think to answer. He rounded the front of the car and dashed through the puddles. "Dear, Lord!" Brian exclaimed as he came upon what he had feared.

Elizabeth Simmons' petite body lay face down in the standing water, wearing what had once been white pajamas. Heavily stained with blood and mixed with water from the puddle, they now appeared pink. Elizabeth's legs were clearly broken, and her outstretched arm rested limply before her. As Brian fell to the saturated earth and knelt at her side, two air bubbles escaped Elizabeth's lips and floated to the water's surface. Brian scooped up her limp body and spun around to face Father Jacob. The old priest held out his arms so Brian could roll Elizabeth into his arms. Her head fell backward, and her body appeared lifeless as Jacob cradled her. With her head tilted back, they could see Elizabeth's throat sliced from her right ear to the middle of her chin. Blood flowed from the wound, and Elizabeth was now unconscious, barely clinging to life.

Brian gripped both sides of his head in a panic as he tried to comprehend what was happening. Then, finally, Jacob yelled, "Brian, take the girl! Get her to the backseat of the sedan!"

As he felt his body stiffen in shock, Brian stood motionless. Jacob shouted louder this time, "TAKE THE GIRL!" Brian snapped out of his trance with a flinch and gingerly removed Elizabeth from Jacob's arms. He tried to process the situation but couldn't rationalize what was happening. Jacob's blue spring jacket was now stained red with young Elizabeth's blood. He had helped his friend into the jacket less than an hour earlier. None of this made any sense.

Brian looked at the attic window and thought, "It's open. No, not open… missing." His eyes shifted from the damaged window to the ground directly below. He could see large pieces of glass embedded in the recently thawed soil, partially submerged in several inches of water.

"Look…up…at the attic window! She must've jumped!" Brian shouted to Jacob.

Father Jacob turned to face the house and saw what Brian was referring to. Elizabeth had apparently shattered the glass in her bedroom window and plunged to the ground.

In a frenzy, Brian exclaimed, "That has to be at least a twenty-foot drop! Dear God in Heaven. Her legs must have shattered when she hit the ground!" Brian questioned, "How did that happen to her throat? What is going on…what happened in that house?"

Jacob shook his head vigorously. "I don't know! My Lord! I don't know! Just please, Brian, let's get her to the backseat and lay her down! Quickly...quickly!"

Brian did as he was told. Jacob followed directly behind him as he glanced back toward the house. Jacob opened the back door for Brian and placed Elizabeth into the dry interior. She showed no reaction to the movement of her broken limbs. Father Jacob slid into the backseat, and Brian ran around the sedan and jumped in. Jacob laid Elizabeth on Brian's lap as he checked in vain for a pulse. Neither Brian nor Jacob knew how to save her or if it was even possible.

Jacob pulled the handkerchief out of his jacket pocket and tried to wrap Elizabeth's wound but life had clearly left her. Brian felt the warmth of her blood on his lap, contrasting with her cold body. Jacob held her small wrist. "Nothing, no pulse." He looked at Brian, who had tears running down his cheeks. There was no way to save her. Elizabeth Simmons was dead.

Rain-soaked and covered in Elizabeth's blood, Brian glanced back at Jacob. He made the Sign of the Cross on her forehead and spoke. "Eternal rest grant unto Elizabeth, O Lord, and let perpetual light shine upon her. May she rest in peace. May almighty God bless us with his peace and strength, the Father and the Son and the Holy Spirit. Amen." After reciting the Last Rites, both men sat for a moment.

So many thoughts were running through Brian's head. He felt such sorrow, such confusion, such pain. He was crying for Elizabeth, crying for all the reasons one mourns the death of a child. But Brian also cried because he hadn't felt anything spiritual take place as he watched her pass on. There had been no evidence of Elizabeth's soul ascending to Heaven. It was the same feeling Brian had when his father finally lost his battle with cancer.

Brian had sat beside his father for two hours after he died, hoping to feel something, hoping for some sign that Heaven was a real place. But he was given no indication on the day of his father's passing or as this precious child's life drained from her body that there was life after death. He didn't know precisely what he had expected to feel or see. Perhaps Brian needed to feel that his father's soul had departed from his body. Maybe he needed a vision of an angel descending from Heaven, ready to carry Elizabeth away. But this had not been the case. Brian only saw cold, dead bodies with eyes as lifeless as Jacob had described the Bunnyman's. As much as he tried to fight the feeling, Brian could feel his faith crumbling, and dark thoughts began emerging from his mind. He knew he had always relied on believing without seeing, but the lack of proof had now overcome his blind faith.

Father Jacob stared at the house looming in the distance. It sat quietly. No movement. No lights. Nothing. His thoughts flashed back to the nightmare Frank had endured. The severity of his situation suddenly hit Jacob like a freight train, and he knew he, too, was being thrust into his own personal nightmare.

"I'll check to see if the car is here. Elizabeth may have been home alone." Brian thought out loud but looked toward Jacob. "If the car is gone, we'll know someone left." Brian opened the door, slid out of the car, and gently placed Elizabeth's head onto the seat, placing Father Jacob's blood-soaked handkerchief over her face. Brian ran to the garage, his pulse accelerating as he turned the door handle. It was locked, but blood rushed to his ears as he stared through the window at the Simmons' Chevrolet. Fear filled every inch of his body.

Father Jacob held Elizabeth's hand as Brian returned to the sedan. "The car is still in the garage, Father. The rest of the family must still be in there." Brian stood up and looked toward the house. It appeared just as it had when they arrived. Motionless and dark.

Brian heard Jacob's door open, and the old priest appeared before him. "Let us head over to the Holt's. We can break the door down and use their phone."

Brian shook his head as he motioned toward the property. "We can't, remember? The Holt's phone line was knocked out in the storm last night." He then said the unthinkable. "The Simmons phone rang when I called earlier, though." Brian pointed to the first-floor windows. "The phone in there is working."

Jacob then knew his fate. Similar to Frank, Jacob would now have to face his own hell. He had preached of it and felt its heat occasionally, but now he was prepared to become fully engulfed in it. He was ready and willing to sacrifice his life to help if necessary, but Jacob knew he needed Brian's help. Asking the same of Brian, who was so much younger and full of life, was almost unbearable.

"I must get into that house and find the phone," Jacob insisted as he faced Brian. "If the family is in there, they need our help. I don't know what is happening, but whatever lies behind those doors, I am prepared. My life's work has led me to this moment. Frank prepared me well. Jesus prepared me well. I am not afraid." He locked his gaze on Brian as he spoke. "You must choose your own path. Leave and go for help if you feel it is right. I am not one to judge your actions. In times of chaos, there is no right or wrong choice." Jacob made his plea known, "But, Brian, I need you now, just as Frank needed me all those years ago."

The choice was obvious to Brian. "I would not leave your side, Father, never. You are my family," Brian pointed to the house, "...and they are as well." He closed the door and walked around the back of the sedan as Father Jacob closed his door, leaving Elizabeth alone in her temporary tomb.

The men stood by each other as they planned their next move. Brian led the quick conversation. "We'll walk through the house together. Everything must be done together, as it's our only advantage." Jacob nodded in agreement. They walked toward the front porch, both lost in their thoughts.

Brian broke the silence. "We should look in the windows before we make our next decision, agreed? Let's not rush into our next move."

Jacob watched for movement in the windows of the

upper levels as they approached the front steps leading to the porch. Then, still looking forward, he answered. "Absolutely. I've been in this house many times. We can see most of the main floor through the front porch windows."

An awful thought suddenly entered Brian's mind. He stopped, grabbed Father Jacob's arm, and questioned him. "Are there any guns in the house? Does Dave hunt? Is it possible that we are walking into an ambush?" He realized they were easy targets for a shooter who may have been watching from inside a dark house.

Jacob tried his best to keep Brian moving forward. "No, Dave was not a hunter, so I do not believe there would be any hunting rifles. As far as a handgun or something for protection, I don't know. I just don't know." He thought about poor Elizabeth's neck. "I don't believe the person who attacked Elizabeth has a gun, though. Remember the girl's neck? A knife did that. If you had a gun, why would you use a knife?"

It was the best conclusion Jacob could come up with. Brian had no choice but to be satisfied. Running his hands through his wet hair, Brian found his courage and walked with Jacob toward the porch. Thankfully, no gunshots were fired in their direction.

They stopped for a moment before ascending the porch steps. Brian went first, slowly, quietly. He stepped up and turned to his right toward the large window he knew would enable them to see into the living room. Then, turning towards Jacob, Brian motioned for him to stop and wait at the top of the steps. Jacob could hardly contain himself from moving forward but obeyed the silent command.

Brian peered through the glass and into a dark, motionless room. He crouched down, turned, and prompted Father Jacob to approach. The old priest crept alongside Brian. Jacob cupped his hands around his eyes and scanned the room behind the glass. No lights were on, and it took a moment for his eyes to adjust to the dark. The room was not tidy, but it was not in disarray as if a struggle had occurred. It looked like a room that had three children living inside its walls.

Jacob could see a staircase leading to the second floor and a partially open door that he recognized led to a bathroom. There was complete silence. Jacob could almost hear it through the glass. Looking at Brian crouching in front of the window, Jacob whispered, "That window will show us the kitchen and dining room." He pointed to the other porch window, past the front door to their left. "Let's check out that side of the house."

Brian arose, and the men stayed close to each other as they made their way to the window. They did not stop to see if the door was unlocked, fearing the noise might startle someone inside. Brian looked first, and then Father Jacob took his turn. Again, nothing to see except an empty house. The kitchen also looked cluttered but not disturbed, and no lights were turned on in any of the rooms.

Brian spoke to Jacob in a hushed voice, pulling him to the right so they were no longer visible if anyone was inside. "The electricity is on in the house. The microwave and stove both have blinking time displays. The power went out sometime this morning, but it's back on now."

Jacob quickly picked up where Brian was headed with his thought and finished it for him. "Which means that there are no lights on in that house, either because it is empty or because someone doesn't want them to be on."

Brian replied, "That's what I'm thinking. Someone could still be in there. The family may still be in there. I don't know."

"There is one more window I would like to check out," Jacob whispered as he pointed to the addition. "Stay here."

Jacob hurried off the porch and made his way to the window that gave him a view into the side addition of the house. He peered into an office. The door to the room was closed, and it, too, stood empty and silent. Jacob returned to the porch and reported his findings to Brian. "No one in there either. From what I remember, that's every room on the first floor. We should be safe down here if we stay together. Let's try the front door."

Brian agreed and pulled the glass storm door as Jacob held it open. Brian's arm was visually shaking as he pushed down on the handle. The door clicked open. He could hear the silence from inside calling to him. Brian quickly, without thinking, closed it again. For a moment, he felt as if he was going to faint.

Brian wanted no more of this. He pulled his hand away from the handle as if it were a hot stovetop and turned to Father Jacob. "What on Earth are we doing here? I can't do this!" He pleaded with Father Jacob. "We need a plan before we walk in there!"

Father Jacob spoke calmly and quietly, trying not to disrupt the silence. "The plan is to get to the telephone and nothing more. First, we head to the kitchen, gather a few knives for protection, and find the phone. Hopefully, it's in the kitchen." Jacob added, "If not, it has to be somewhere on this level. I'll lead the way to the kitchen, so stay close to me. Look for a phone as we pass through the living room. Stay together, though. If you see a phone, don't go to it. Let's get the knives first. Also, do not turn on any lights. Let's keep our presence in the house a secret if possible."

Brian reluctantly agreed as Jacob finished. "We'll find what we need if we stay calm." He concluded the plan. "If the phone is dead, we return immediately to the sedan and seek help. If it works, we call 911 and then return to the sedan. Whatever happened here looks to have happened on one of the upper floors. There will be no need to stay in the house longer than needed. We will wait for the police from inside the car. My heart is not strong enough to witness more horror and brutality today." Jacob looked at his own trembling hands. "I must leave this family's fate to God." He placed his hand on Brian's shoulder and looked at him with old eyes, the flames burning low. "I am just a man; we are just men out of our element. We are not capable of intervening any further. We will wait, and pray, and hope."

Both priests were now feeling immense pressure and fear. Brian's self-doubt was beginning to overtake him. What monsters could be lurking in the shadows, under the beds, in the basement, in the closets? The house was still so dark. Brian remembered the drawn blinds on some of the second-floor windows. He thought of how dark those rooms would be. "What is lurking in that impossible silence inside the darkness of those rooms? Maybe the Bunnyman? Maybe my mother? Maybe the Devil? Maybe Jesus Christ?"

Father Jacob also felt fear. He had felt all types of fear throughout his life. He had survived the horrors of war. He had been shot at in the middle of the night by strangers wanting to kill him. He had survived bombs falling from the sky. He had felt fear of taking his oath to God, becoming a priest responsible for saving souls. He felt fear of moving to an unknown town to preach the Gospel. Jacob had felt fear when being accused of crimes he did not commit. He had felt the fear in Frank's voice for all those years as he spoke of Johnny Boy...the Bunnyman. He felt the fear of growing old and leaving his congregation. He still feared being alone at the end of his life, but he was wise and knew that on the other side of fear lay freedom.

Jacob knew there was little he could do for the Simmons family, but fear could not stop him from trying to help.

Chapter Fourteen

Brian turned towards the door and grabbed the handle again. "We must do this, and we do it now." A rush of adrenaline overtook him when he thought of how Frank must have felt entering the cellar, fearing the Bunnyman lurking in the darkness. Brian had to move. "This will be over in just a few minutes. Let's get this done and put it behind us. For the sake of the family and our sanity." He spoke a bit louder now, sternly to Jacob and himself, ashamed at having doubts. Finally, he turned his head towards Jacob and winked, nodding as he spoke. "For Frank."

The fire in Father Jacob's eyes blazed once again. To hear Frank's name spoken aloud was the fuel to spark the dying embers. It was the fuel he needed to keep this hellfire lit. If Frank could survive his nightmare, they could as well. He braced for whatever lay on the other side of the door and nodded to Brian. He was ready.

Brian pressed down on the handle and slowly opened the door. He could feel the house sucking him in. The silence was not going to let them get away. Jacob stood directly to his right as Brian pushed the door open. It swung into an empty room, stopping when it hit a coffee table along the wall. Before they stepped through the threshold, they scanned the interior for a few seconds, looking and listening.

Nothing moved, and no gunshots were fired. No one attacked them with a knife. To their astonishment, the house smelled delightful. It was impossible to ignore the recent activity in the kitchen. The aroma of the Easter meal preparation still lingered in the air. Life had seemingly carried on as usual in this house not too long ago. The silence was incomplete, though, as they could hear the refrigerator humming in the kitchen. The furnace also emitted a low rumble as warm air flowed through the vents.

Sticking to their plan, Jacob led Brian slowly through the living room towards the kitchen doorway. Out of habit, Brian closed the front door behind him as he searched the room for any signs of a phone. He did not see one at first glance. Brian couldn't believe how ordinary everything looked and smelled. Everything would have seemed normal had a dead girl not dropped out of one of the attic windows. He cursed himself for such an awful thought.

The priests passed into the kitchen. On the right wall, a set of glass French doors stood open. They presented a clear view into the adjoining dining room. Still, nothing moved, but then the floor vibrated for a second. The men paused as the air in the vents stopped moving. "That was just the furnace turning off." Father Jacob whispered to Brian. Now the only sound to be heard, saving them from complete silence, was the soft humming of the refrigerator.

Brian was the one who spotted the knife block sitting on the far counter. He grabbed Father Jacob by the arm and pointed to where it sat. It had been blocked from view when they had looked into the window a few minutes earlier. The block was tipped over; all its contents had been spilled onto the countertop. Brian walked to where it lay and stood the block upright. He immediately returned the knives to their slots to see how many were missing. It was evident the three biggest slots would remain empty.

Brian stumbled backward after he had put the last knife in place. Father Jacob, who had kept his distance, caught Brian and let him rest momentarily. Then, after Brian's legs regained strength, Jacob let go, placed both hands on Brian's shoulders, and asked, "How many are missing?"

"It looks like the three biggest knives are gone," Brian replied in disbelief. "All the steak knives and smaller ones are here." A thought then occurred to him. "They could have been put somewhere else. We should check the sink and the drawers."

A hasty search was done throughout the kitchen. As he searched, Jacob thought of Elizabeth. One of those missing knives had been used to cut her neck. He had no doubts about that.

Neither the missing knives nor a telephone was found. Brian located some larger knives in a drawer, but they did not match the slots in the block. He grabbed two of the steak knives for their own protection. "These are extremely sharp, Father," Brian cautioned as he handed one to Jacob, "Please be careful in the darkness."

Father Jacob accepted the knife from Brian. He needed this nightmare to end. "Please, let's find the telephone quickly. I didn't see one in the living room. We must still check the dining room, office, and bathroom." Jacob led them through the French doors into the dining room.

The priests immediately noticed a charging cradle for a cordless phone on an antique end table. Much to their disappointment, the phone was not on the charger. Brian cursed loudly to himself as he turned to face Jacob. "Damn, the phone isn't on the charger." he sighed in discouragement, "Let's search the office."

Jacob led them through the kitchen and back into the living room when suddenly he stopped. Something was different. They both noticed the change at the same time. The hum of the refrigerator was no longer there. It had turned off during the few minutes they had searched the dining room. The house was now utterly silent. The two priests held their breath momentarily, too scared to make the air move in front of them. They feared even the sound of their own breathing would upset the balance of the house and their sanity.

As they reached the office door, Jacob remembered it had appeared empty from the outside. He turned the knob and quickly pushed the door open. The sound of creaking hinges broke the house's silence. Father Jacob turned to face the living room, expecting the end to come, but nothing changed. The slight interruption in the house's silence did not wake any slumbering beasts. Everything in the house remained as it was. There was no movement, only silence once again.

Brian pushed past Jacob. "I'll take a quick look in here." He entered the office as Jacob stood in the doorway and waited. Scanning the living room, Jacob could barely see the bathroom door from where he stood. Without thinking, he made his way toward the bathroom, hoping to bring an end to their search a bit faster. Jacob reached the hallway entrance but lacked the courage to cross through it. He wondered what lay where he could not see. Jacob backed up into the safety of the living room.

Brian stepped out of the office, shaking his head. He met Jacob in the middle of the room. "No phone in there either." As Brian glanced at the elderly priest, defeat, yet relief could be seen in Jacob's eyes. Brian spoke in a whisper again. "I don't know what else can be done, Father. It seems there is nothing more we can safely do here."

Jacob pointed to the bathroom and whispered, "I would still like to look in there before we leave." He hung his head as if in shame. 'I was too scared to cross the hall without you."

Brian nodded. "A few more seconds." he thought to himself. "Just a few steps deeper into this madness." He agreed. "O.K. Let's do it then."

The men approached the bathroom, gripping their knives as if expecting to be attacked from unseen corners. The windowless hallway turned to the right revealing an open staircase climbing over the bathroom. Brian poked his head around the corner to make sure it was empty. Feeling safe enough to proceed, they made their way across the hall.

Jacob pushed the bathroom door open with his left hand, still gripping the knife tightly with his right. The door swung open, exposing the small bathroom. There was no need to enter the room as it was apparent that the phone was not in there. The only objects in the otherwise empty space were a toilet, mirror, and sink.

The two priests stood alone in the dark hallway, their agreed-upon search complete. Both felt hopeless and defeated but ready to escape. Brian looked at Jacob and motioned his head toward the front door. They turned to leave. Anything else that needed to be said could be spoken outside. That's when they heard the boy.

A gut-wrenching sob descended from the top of the staircase. The silence of the house had been shattered. It was a short burst of sound, but it was enough to awaken every monster, devil, and demon lurking inside the house's shadows.

Brian spoke in a frantic whisper. "Was that J.J.?"

Jacob whipped around and faced the open stairs. "It most certainly was."

With a newfound sense of urgency and purpose, Jacob raced to the base of the staircase and listened, but nothing more was heard. Finally, he returned to Brian and stated, "I cannot leave the child. I must go to him. You can return to the car if you wish, but I must continue. Going after J.J. involves great risk, but it is my calling."

The young priest's mind raced as he came to terms with what was happening. He had heard the boy's wail, and he had heard Jacob's intentions. This was not his imagination playing cruel tricks. This was reality, no matter how far gone it seemed. He looked into Jacob's eyes, hoping for an answer. There was no longer fear in them. Instead, Brian saw two flames burning intensely. The flame of God...the flame of the Lord. It was clear that Jacob had given himself completely. He was not leaving the house without that child.

The only fire in Brian was fueled by terror… tremendous fear. Where was his salvation? He saw nothing of Christ or God in this waking nightmare. Brian felt pitiful and weak, frightened of devils, frightened of death, frightened by the evil of humanity.

Jacob snapped Brian back to reality with a question. "What do you want to do?"

Brian knew there was no other choice. Jacob would go with or without him. "Where you go, I go, Father." He bowed his head in defeat. "There is no other way." He had not only given himself completely, but he had also now given up completely. Brian had no choice but to do as Father Jacob instructed. He understood the horrors held within the Simmons house would offer no escape for them. They no longer had free will; their paths had been predestined.

If this were the end, Brian decided his final act would be an attempt to save J.J. The new goal gave him renewed strength. He looked back at Jacob and held his finger to his lips. "As much as you want to, DON'T call out to the boy," Brian whispered forcefully, "Don't give up our position. I'll lead us up the steps. Keep your knife pointed down, O.K.?" Jacob nodded, ready to move.

Brian slowly walked around to the base of the staircase with Jacob in tow. They looked to the top of the steps and saw no one. The second-level hallway was completely dark; the only light source came from windows inside the adjoining rooms.

Brian and Jacob began the climb upward. The creaking of the hardwood was inevitable, and there wasn't anything they could do about it. After they ascended halfway up, Brian could look into the hallway above. He could see a small landing to the right that was not visible from the first floor. Brian saw a doorway and another stairwell that he assumed would lead to the attic. He stopped Father Jacob and crawled up several more steps on his hands and knees. When Brian's head was at floor level, he glanced around the corner, up the stairwell to the attic, and then down the hallway. The dim gray daylight was enough to see that both directions were clear. He rose, climbed to the top step, and gestured for Jacob to follow.

Together the men stepped onto the second level, pausing to listen. They heard nothing but the howling of the wind. Jacob squinted as he focused his eyes on the stairwell that led to the attic. The day's gray tone was prominent in the room above. He remembered the broken window, the young girl's neck, and J.J.'s sob. Jacob began his ascent to the attic without waiting for Brian's approval.

Seeing Jacob's break from the plan, Brian raced up the staircase. He could feel anger arise within. "What is he doing?" Brian thought.

Jacob was standing at the top of the steps looking into the room when Brian caught up to him. Anger was quickly replaced with questions and fear. "Was the boy up here? Was the killer?" Brian glanced around the room, relieved to see that they were alone.

Brian's nerves settled for the moment. The attic was a spacious area without closets or adjoining rooms. Two windows provided enough light to see clearly. Still, Brian avoided looking at the damaged window as he surveyed the surroundings. As he investigated, he whispered to Jacob, "Watch the stairway while I take a quick look around."

Father Jacob obeyed the command as Brian moved throughout the room. Brian froze upon seeing Elizabeth's bed. Fresh blood covered her pillowcase and sheets. Brian's eyes followed the blood trail as it reached the broken window. Bloody handprints could be seen on the frame and the wall surrounding it. Shattered glass and wood fragments lay on the floor below the window. A small wooden chair was standing upright on top of the debris. It, too, was stained with the bloody handprints of a child.

Brian whispered to Jacob. "It is clear to me now…come…look." Brian first pointed to the bed and then to the floor. His finger shook as it pointed to the blood trail out the window.

Jacob rushed to where Brian was pointing and stood before the broken window. "Elizabeth must have been attacked in her bed. Someone tried to cut her throat as she slept." Brian said the words but could not comprehend the brutality. "She must have woken up during the assault and fought for her life. The poor girl managed to break open the window and climb out." Brian continued his analysis. "To do this, she must have subdued her attacker. Perhaps she fought back with that chair? Maybe she was being kept prisoner until she bled to death?" Brian shook his head, "I just don't know. She must have been trapped up here, though. For whatever reason, she chose to jump out of the window instead of running down the steps. It must have happened very quickly. I wonder how long she was lying out there in the rain?"

The bottom edge of the window was slightly below Jacob's chest as he looked through the fragmented glass. The sky to the north was still filled with storm clouds, but he could see an orange haze emitting from their blackness. To the south, the sun was fighting to return to the day. Jacob looked down to the ground, attempting to grasp the height of the fall. The standing water was slowly being absorbed by the earth below. As he scanned the area where Elizabeth had landed, Jacob's eyes rested upon an item that sent chills down his spine. "Oh, my God! Dear Lord in Heaven!" Jacob pointed toward the ground. Brian followed Jacob's finger line to the lawn below. A look of defeat overcame his face.

Brian stared at the ground briefly and then pulled his eyes from the window. Finally, one mystery had been solved. In the yard, directly below them, amongst pieces of broken glass, lay the missing cordless phone. Elizabeth had jumped out of the window holding it.

It all made too much horrific sense. The phone was hidden from view when they first found Elizabeth but had now been revealed by the receding water.

Chapter Fifteen

Brian and Jacob had ventured too deep into this nightmare. It had fully consumed them, and no more needed to be said of the phone. Both men now focused on what lay below them...to the boy...to freedom. Brian quickly formed a new plan and repeated it to Jacob. "I remember seeing several doors on the second floor. One of them was open. Let's check out the room with the open door first. If J.J.'s not in there, we'll go back to the first door on the left and work our way down the hall. This will lessen the possibility of being caught off guard by someone exiting from an unopened door." As much as he hated to, Brian had to state the obvious. "No matter what we find inside these rooms, remember that J.J.'s our priority. We know he's alive, but I have little hope for the others."

Jacob added, "Yes, my son, I agree; this situation looks grim. I am prepared to do what I must, to see what my eyes must see. I know that there is no escaping what lies ahead. We will move forward with the Lord by our sides." There was no fear in his voice. "Let us say a prayer before we proceed. Please, Brian, recite with me."

The two Priests recited Psalms 57:1 and 140:4. "Have mercy on me, my God, have mercy on me, for in you I take refuge. I will take refuge in the shadow of your wings until the disaster has passed. Keep me safe, LORD, from the hands of the wicked; protect me from the violent, who devise ways to trip my feet... Amen." They each made the Sign of the Cross and descended unknowingly into the depths of hell.

As the men returned to the second floor, their eyes adjusted to the house's darkness. They could see to the end of the hall, and the second door on the left stood open just as Brian had remembered. The hallway remained undisturbed, and a patch of dull gray daylight made its way into the darkness as it penetrated the translucent cloth curtains inside the room with the open door.

Brian pointed to the door and then to himself, gesturing to Jacob to stand behind him. They made their way down the hall, back to back, knives drawn, expecting an attack. Jacob watched the closed doors and stairwell for movement. Brian braced for whatever exposed itself from the open door. He saw no movement in the gray light as he inched closer to the room.

As Brian turned to enter the open room, his heart leaped from his chest! The killer stood directly before him. He backed into the hallway, bracing for an assault, throwing his entire body in position to shield Jacob. Brian's heart raced as he waited for the inevitable attack. When none came, Brian gathered his courage and slowly glanced around the corner into the small room. Relief washed over him as he realized what he thought to be the killer had only been a reflection of himself in the bathroom mirror. He shook his head and waved his hand at Jacob, whose face was white as a ghost. Brian took a deep breath and proceeded into the bathroom.

Brian's heart was still racing as he entered the small room. Jacob followed close behind, color slowly returning to his face. Next to the vanity stood a toilet, and an antique claw foot tub sat along the right wall with a window directly above. The dull light through the curtain made the room look bland. All colors had been erased and replaced with shades of black, white, and gray. One step into the room proved there was no need to go further. The sight that lay before them was repulsive.

The middle-child, Michael, lay partially face down inside the claw foot tub. His head, torso, and arms were out of view, but his hips balanced his body on the tub's rim, and his lifeless legs hung out. The tops of his feet and shins rested on the floor. The shower curtain had been ripped down and shoved inside the bathtub with his body. Blood splatter, which appeared black in the colorless room, covered the walls and floor.

Brian ripped open the curtains on the window above, thinking the light of the day would somehow make this horror disappear. It did not. It only made the scene more realistic; more detailed. Now the colors were vivid. Michael's blood was as red and as fresh as Elizabeth's. Brian dropped to his knees and sobbed in agony.

Jacob quickly turned to look away. The few moments he had glimpsed into the room were enough. He saw the slaughter that had taken place and recognized the similarities to the work of a butcher. There was no hope for the boy. Jacob returned to the hallway's darkness and closed his eyes, but it was too late. He had seen what could not be unseen.

Attempting to compose himself, Brian reached for the side of the toilet and pulled himself up. Extreme paranoia had taken control of his mind, and he longed to escape this house of death. Brian looked back at Jacob and again stated the obvious. "Michael is dead. All we can do for the boy is pray for his soul."

Father Jacob covered his face with both hands and moaned in agony. He could not contain himself as every moment inside this house seemed consumed with tragedy. Jacob could sense a sinister presence lurking in the shadows...just as Frank had...so many years ago.

Brian closed his eyes and turned to face the horrific scene. He raised his hand toward Michael's frail body. In unison, the men whispered Psalm 23. "The LORD is my shepherd..." After their prayer, they made the cross sign in the air toward Michael's body.

Brian then turned and gently pushed Jacob back toward the stairs to the first door on the left. J.J. could still be alive, so they had to press on. The men would check the next room and then move across the hallway if necessary. They stood before the closed door, where Brian could tell the window blinds had been pulled down in the room. No daylight escaped from under this door as it did from the door across the hall.

For an instant, Brian recalled the talk Jacob had with Frank about the soul and thought to himself, "Was it possible that all souls could be saved? What about the soul of the monster that had killed these children? What about a soul that was entirely dark and filled with nothing but pure evil? How could a soul so black not be sent deep into the pits of hell to suffer for all eternity?" It was clear to Brian that some souls could not be saved. You could only pray for death.

Brian placed his left hand on the doorknob and held the knife with his right. The door would swing open to his left, and he wanted to be ready for an attack. Jacob stood to the right of the door with his back against the wall, watching the two doors across the hall...listening. The house was still so silent, and Jacob wondered. "Was the cry we heard earlier our imaginations? Did we actually hear J.J.?" He was no longer thinking clearly. "Wasn't it just a few hours ago I was standing in front of my beloved congregation, basking in the love and goodness of humanity? Look where I am now. What is this place?" Jacob concluded that it had to be hell.

Jacobs' thoughts were interrupted when he noticed Brian frantically waving his arms to get Jacob's attention. He blinked a few times to regain focus on the young priest. Brian gestured for Jacob to stay back until the door was open, mouthing that Jacob should follow him and guard the doorway as Brian secured the room. Jacob slowly nodded, not fully comprehending what Brian had tried to say.

Brian swung open the door with a deep breath and quickly returned to the hallway behind the wall's protection. His left foot unintentionally stepped onto the wood of the top step of the staircase. Brian realized that if they were attacked from inside the room or from one of the closed doors, it would be easy for him to flee the house. He could sprint down the stairs and straight through the front door. With a sinking feeling, Brian realized he had left Father

Jacob alone in the hallway to be ambushed. "Did I do this intentionally?" Brian felt nauseated as he questioned, "What kind of a sick person has these thoughts?" Brian promised himself he would not run. No matter what horror came out of the room, he was NOT a coward… Brian would never leave Jacob.

No movement or sound came from within the room. Brian quickly glanced down the staircase to the first-floor landing and saw no one. Daylight streamed in from the windows below. Shadows came and went as clouds passed over the sun's rays. Brian turned his head toward the open door and closed his eyes. He listened carefully as his pupils adjusted to the darkness behind his eyelids, expecting the room to be pitch black. It was in this blackness that Brian expected to be attacked. He opened his eyes, glanced at Jacob, and cautiously entered the room.

Jacob followed Brian through the door as instructed. He watched Brian take a few steps into the blackness, wielding his knife before him. A sliver of light peeked from the edge of the window blind. Jacob slid to his left and kept tight to the wall, gripping his knife firmly.

A few seconds passed, and the priests had not been ambushed. The room remained silent, and there was no movement. Brian quickly turned in a circle, trying to see every corner of the large bedroom. No one hid in the shadows or behind the door. He saw an unopened closet and was sure there was enough room under the bed for someone to hide. Brian turned to Jacob and then glanced out of the doorway to the hall. Again, there was nothing but silence. He went to the nearest window and pulled back the heavy curtain, letting dreary daylight flood the room. Brian looked back at Jacob and focused on the dim reflection in his weary eyes.

Jacob had a look of dread etched on his face, fear burning hot from behind his stare. Brian followed Jacob's gaze and turned to face the room's newly lit interior. Brian put his hands to his head and tightly squeezed his eyes shut, hoping what lay before him would disappear when he opened them. Brian's body was on fire, and sweat consumed him. His head pounded, and the room spun. Tears began to fall from the corners of his eyes.

Brian opened his swollen eyes to see his friend, David Simmons, lying in his king-size bed. From a distance, it would have appeared as if Dave was sleeping. His body looked undisturbed as he faced the ceiling. But Brian had noticed the pool of blood around Dave's head. Brian's eyes followed the blood trail from Dave's pillow to his cheek and then to his left eye socket. That's when he saw the knife. Dave must have been stabbed as he slept; the blade jabbed through his closed eyelid. His right eye was open, staring up at the ceiling. A milky blue haze filled the dilated pupil. Brian recognized the knife handle and looked at the one he held in his hand. Both had been removed from the same knife block downstairs.

Brian stood in shock as he listened to Jacob's weeping in the shadows behind him. In his despair, Brian could not think of what to say. He turned with his head bowed as a large stain on the carpet caught his eye, and he immediately knew it was blood. In his paranoia, Brian whipped around, sure someone or something was behind him. Yet nothing stood in the silent room, and he returned his focus to Jacob. Brian pointed toward the blood stain on the carpet.

Through his tears, the old priest looked at what Brian was referring to. Jacob saw the blood stain but also noticed more blood trailing on the carpet before him. Someone had bled in that spot but then moved. In desperation, Jacob pleaded with Brian. "Where is Cindy? Do you think she could have escaped?"

Brian's thoughts raced back to the time he and Jacob spent outside the house. "Did we miss seeing her when we were outside...like we missed the phone?" He ran over to the window facing the front of the house and set his knife on the ledge. As he pulled the blind, it snapped to the top and fell halfway down again before resting. Brian pushed the sagging blind up and bent down to look outside. The water continued to recede, and the sun had taken control of the sky to the south. The storm clouds fled fast, moving out of sight to the north. Brian only saw the empty driveway and sedan below. He looked in both directions as far as the window allowed but did not see anyone.

Suddenly Jacob called, "My God, Brian, look to your right!" He could barely utter the words. "There is blood all over the wall!"

Brian dropped the window blind, stood, and turned. He looked down to the side of the bed and saw the sheets and comforter hanging off the mattress, forming a heap on the floor. Blood was splattered on the side of the mattress and covered the bed frame, nightstand, and walls. Just then, Brian saw a motionless body only a few feet away.

Cindy was tangled up among the blankets on the

floor. Brian could see she was face down, lying on her stomach. Her head rested on its right cheek facing the wall. There were no visible injuries to Cindy's head, but the bed sheets around her torso were stained heavily with bright red blood. Brian could make out several puncture wounds to her back through the thin layers of her t-shirt and the bed sheets. Cindy's arms were free from the twisted mess and were stretched outward. Her right hand was frozen in a death grip on one of the legs of her nightstand. On top of the nightstand stood another cordless phone. The chord that connected the phone's cradle to the wall had been cut, rendering it useless. Cindy's other hand had been anchored to the floor just below her thumb and index finger with another of the missing kitchen knives.

Jacob could not see Cindy's body with his back against the wall beside the doorway. He had only noticed the blood-stain. Jacob watched as Brian stumbled across the room. Jacob rushed toward Brian, but in doing so, he caught a glimpse of blonde hair and an outstretched left arm next to the bed. Knowing that the arm belonged to Cindy, Jacob stumbled backward, using the wall to break his fall. He closed his eyes and made the Sign of the Cross as he silently prayed.

Too light-headed and weak to stand, Brian sat on the window sill for a moment, staring at his deceased friends. He could feel the warmth from the sunshine on his back. The storm was now a memory, but it had carried them deep into a nightmare…down into the depths of hell. The only hope that Brian had left was to find the young boy and get him out alive. Somehow, he found the strength to stand up but knew he must pray for Dave and Cindy.

Brian looked to Jacob, who was whispering a silent prayer. He watched the shadows outside the room, wondering how much time they had left. The only movement he saw was of Father Jacob's arm making the Sign of the Cross as he finished his prayer.

"Please, Father, I have to pray for their souls before we leave." Brian spoke as the old priest's eyes opened. "Dave and Cindy were so kind to me. We became friends the first day I arrived in town. Dave was waiting at St. James when I drove into the parking lot for the first time. The two of you showed me around. Do you remember, Father? I liked Dave; so easygoing and kind. Cindy was my friend, too, and the children, what beautiful children." With hunched shoulders, Brian began to weep. "I need a few moments with each of my friends."

Jacob closed his eyes as he rested his head against the wall. "Of course, I remember that day. It was a special day for me as well. We became friends that day too." Jacob smiled weakly at Brian. "Take the time you need, my son. I will rest my eyes here and listen for any sound in the hallway." Even with everything that had just occurred, the old priest felt he could fall asleep instantly. He was exhausted both physically and emotionally.

Brian approached Cindy and kneeled between her body and the bed. Sunlight was streaming through the windows, fully illuminating Cindy's body. Brian touched her shoulder, noticing how cold she felt under the sun's warmth. Dave was lying on the far side of the bed, so Brian decided to pray for Cindy first. He would then pray for Dave...just as he had done with their children. He felt an obligation to help free their souls from this horrible place.

A place the family had once lovingly called "Home."

Chapter Sixteen

Jacob first heard the nursery rhyme coming from the hallway. "I must be dreaming. This is just another part of this twisted nightmare." Jacob's thoughts seemed so distant, and his eyes were still closed, but he distinctly heard the faint, muffled sound of child-like singing.

"Here comes Peter Cottontail, hopping down the bunny trail...hippity hoppity, Easter's on its way." Jacob could not believe what he was hearing. He had to be dreaming, but a moment later, the song repeated, "Here comes Peter Cottontail, hopping down the bunny trail...hippity hoppity, Easter's on its way."

Jacob's eyes flew open. Brian was still on the floor with Cindy, and he could see Dave's lifeless body on the bed. If Jacob had been dreaming, he was awake now. The song repeated for a third time. "Here comes Peter Cottontail, Hopping down the bunny trail..." Jacob spun into the hallway, his knife drawn. "...hippity hoppity, Easter's on its way."

The singing became louder as Jacob entered the hallway. Jacob glanced back at Brian. He was still by Cindy's side and appeared oblivious to the strange singing. Jacob quickly scanned the staircase but saw no one. The door across the hall was closed, so he turned to face the far end of the hallway.

Jacob then heard it a fourth time. The singing was

louder than when he was in the bedroom, but the words were still muffled. He could hear the song coming from behind the closed door at the end of the hall. At that moment, Jacob forgot about Dave, Cindy, and even Father Brian. The melody entranced him, and his only thought was that the singing would lead him to J.J.

As in a dream, the old priest followed the tune. Appearing to be a beacon from God, the light from the bathroom window shone into the hallway, illuminating the closed door. Jacob thought, "The boy must be in that room!" Jacob praised the Lord and knew this was a moment of Divine Intervention. He was confident the Lord was showing him the way. Jacob made his way down the hall but stopped as he heard the sound of a door handle. Subtly, the door at the end of the hall appeared to open on its own. After opening only a crack, it stopped, so Jacob could not see into the room. He stood frozen in place as the glowing rays of sunlight invited him further in.

Jacob heard the song again, clearly this time. "Here comes Peter Cottontail, Hopping down the bunny trail...hippity hoppity, Easter's on its way." He quickly continued to the far end of the hall. Jacob saw himself in the mirror as he passed the bathroom, and death stared back at him. He had not noticed until then, but his cassock and jacket were stained red with blood. His face was pale, wrinkled, and filled with sorrow. Moaning as he turned away, he again focused on finding J.J. His appearance meant nothing to him. Jacob stood only momentarily in front of the door. The sunlight from the hallway patiently awaited its entry into the room, falling upon the old priest's back.

The song played again. This time it was directly in front of Jacob. "Here comes Peter Cottontail..." With the Lord by his side, he was unafraid as his hand moved toward the door.

"...hopping down the bunny trail..."

Jacob held his knife pointed to the floor in his left hand. He pushed on the door with the other. The sunlight swept into the room as the door swung open.

"...hippity, hoppity, Easter's on its way."

Father Jacob encountered a mechanical, stuffed Easter Bunny lying on the floor only a few feet into the room. It was built to be upright, meant to walk, but it was now lying on its back, facing the ceiling. The toy rocked from side to side on the floor as its arms and legs moved back and forth. Jacob's body blocked the toy from the sunlight. In his shadow, he saw rotating pastel colors projecting from the toy's stomach and ears.

Jacob looked up from the toy and deeper into the room. He saw the boy sitting on a small bed before him, positioned sideways along the opposite wall. The child sat with his legs in a cross-legged position and held a large Easter basket in his lap. A fluffy white Easter Bunny headband sat on his head, and he appeared angelic in the soft glow of the sunlight. Jacob focused only on the child's eyes as J.J. squinted into the sunlight. Relief filled every square inch of Jacob's frail body as he stumbled into the room, kicking the toy bunny to the side. "Praise the Lord; he is alright!" Father Jacob's mind shouted the words but did not say them for fear of startling the child.

J.J. gazed upon the floor where his toy had sat but was distracted by Jacob's approaching shadow.

Slowly, the bedroom door closed, forcing the cleansing rays of daylight back into the hallway. No light remained in the boy's cruel sanctuary, and the waiting darkness devoured Jacob's shadow. So many thoughts occurred to him at once that Jacob's reeling mind did not comprehend the change.

The old priest tried to speak but was unable to find his voice. Jacob bent to one knee, set his knife on the floor, and outstretched his arms toward the child. The boy remained unresponsive, almost as if under a spell. Jacob understood now that J.J. would need to be carried out of the house.

Struggling to stand, Jacob felt a burning in his chest. He found it nearly impossible to approach the bed. When he was finally able to speak, he managed only a whisper and spoke between measured breaths. "Come, my son…I will take you away from here. Let us walk…and feel the sunshine on our faces." Jacob spoke his last words to spite his vile surroundings. "This…is no place…for a child of the Lord."

Jacob reached past the boy's Easter basket attempting to grab J.J. by the waist. As he extended his arms, Jacob suddenly recoiled in terror. He stood up straight and stepped back in shock. Jacob's senses flooded with hopelessness and terror as he stared at the grotesque tragedy. He could now smell the odor of death and decay as it hung stagnant in the air. The bitter taste of bile rose from his stomach as nausea overtook him. He could feel his chest tighten as his arm and jaw began to ache.

A gravelly voice snarled from somewhere in the blackness. "You are correct, Father, this is NOT a place for your Lord," The voice grew louder, "…or for one of his pathetic disciples." Jacob's heart could take no more. He twisted his body to face the monstrous voice. A man's dark silhouette, similar to his own, emerged from the shadows as he continued to mock the old priest. "It seems you have tread too far into the darkness, Jacob." The vile voice was somehow familiar. "I am quite positive the shadows will not allow you to leave."

Jacob clenched his chest with both hands. Managing only one step forward, he inadvertently kicked his knife across the room. He could hear it bounce as it hit the carpet, disappearing forever into the deepening layers of darkness. The man flashed Jacob a devilish grin through the gloom. A wave of disbelief swept over the old priest. He knew this man. He recognized the familiar stare of death.

In an instant, Jacob's muscles began to spasm and cramp. The blood in his veins flowed like molten metal. Sweat poured from his face as his clothes clung to his skin. He staggered into the darkness, thinking only of putting distance between himself and this ungodly man.

Jacob caught himself in the corner of the room. He attempted to brace his body with his head and shoulders, but his legs would no longer hold him. Jacob fell backward into the darkness like a ship's mast snapping in the wind. Flashes of light exploded inside his head as he hit the floor. Once again, the darkness then engulfed him.

Lying on his back, Jacob inhaled and exhaled with great effort. His lungs ached for oxygen in a room that wanted his last breath. He heard the man amble towards him from somewhere in the abyss. The old priest would not allow his final moments to be shared with such evil. Using his remaining strength, Jacob turned away from the footsteps and onto his side. His long body naturally curled into the fetal position. The stuffed bunny lay on its side, facing him.

Jacob's kick had damaged the toy. Its arms and legs barely moved, and the bunny no longer sang its song. The light inside its belly was dim, but Jacob focused on the steady swirling of pastel colors and prayed. The old priest's body relaxed, and he could smell the aroma of the Holy incense he had burnt during the morning's mass. The smoke had penetrated his clothing while he had blessed his congregation. Jacob could feel their presence inside him, and the love he felt set his soul at ease. He was at peace, smiling as his senses began to fade.

Jacob felt the force of a kick to his back but suffered no pain. He heard the wretched man's voice for only a moment before it faded. The light inside the toy's belly began to grow in brilliance. The pastel colors spiraled in a radiant glow. The swirling quickened until the aura became one brilliant shimmering diamond.

The light expanded outward from the toy and began to fill the room. It fed off itself, growing more intense as it propelled away the darkness. Jacob was encompassed inside the purity of the diamond. As the warm light washed over him, he felt secure in the Lord's embrace. The old priest forgot about his senses and the suffering that they brought.

Jacob forgot about his earthly body, and then he, too, became the light.

Chapter Seventeen

Brian kneeled in silence. When he regained strength, he reached onto the bed and pulled himself to a standing position. A flash of fear washed over him as he realized he'd forgotten to check under the bed. Brian quickly lowered himself to the floor and glanced underneath. He took a deep breath and put his forehead on the floor, relaxing only when he saw the other side of the room.

As Brian's head rested on the floor of Dave and Cindy's bedroom, he realized he did not see Jacob's feet along the far wall. Pulling himself into a kneeling position, Brian noticed that Jacob was no longer in the room. He called out to Jacob, but there was no reply. Brian stood up too quickly, and the room began to spin. While sitting on the edge of the bed for a moment to regain his balance, Brian instinctively reached for Dave's hand. He whispered a prayer hoping that David's soul was on its way to a better place.

Brian sat upright on the bed and scanned the room for any sign of Jacob. He ran to the closet door and swung it open but found no one hiding inside. Brian looked out to the yard for any activity but saw no one. Retrieving his knife from the window ledge, he now felt utterly alone.

Brian entered the hallway and noticed both previously unopened doors remained closed, and the stairs and hallway were empty. Brian wondered, "Did Jacob run out on me?" Brian helplessly spun around in the hallway. Fear again had overtaken him, and he seemed to have lost all willpower. Brian wanted to run out of the house screaming, but something kept him from doing so. Instead, without further thought, he turned to the unopened door closest to him and opened it.

This door led to another bedroom with open blinds that allowed daylight to fill the space. Thankfully, there were no signs of blood or a struggle. Brian could tell he was in Michael's room. Posters of famous bands and swimsuit models were tacked to the walls. Clothes were sprawled in piles throughout, and empty dishes and open packages of food rested on the top of the dresser. A small T.V. with a PlayStation 2 sat in a small entertainment center. Brian knew the room at the end of the hall must be J.J.'s. It had to be.

Brian imagined the entire scene that must have taken place. "When the power was out, the intruder entered the house. Dave and Cindy were attacked first, and Dave was stabbed in the eye while he slept. Cindy awoke and tried to escape but was attacked as she tried to flee the bed. Michael must have woken up from the chaos in his parent's bedroom and, without knowing, walked into the slaughter. Michael was assaulted inside the door, so blood was splattered on the floor in Dave and Cindy's bedroom. He was murdered next to his parents and then carried to the bathroom."

Brian shuddered as he continued his thought process. "Because Elizabeth was in the attic, she must not have heard the commotion. She would have still been sleeping as she was attacked. The poor girl awoke and fought off her attacker but was trapped in the attic. She tried to use the phone, but it would not have worked. Elizabeth must have known she would bleed to death without help, so she had no choice but to break the window and jump."

Only young J.J. remained, and Brian would do whatever it took to save the child. Brian left Michael's room, turned to his right, and faced the far end of the hallway. He noticed how perfectly the sun's rays outlined J.J.'s bedroom door, just as Jacob had. Brian, too, had the notion of Divine Intervention. The light from outside was so much brighter than the shadows within the house. In Brian's fragile state of mind, the sun's rays also appeared as a guiding light.

Brian walked down the hall to the last room on the right. As he made his way, he thought, "Why was this happening? What was the reason, the purpose for any of this? A whole family slaughtered on Easter of all days? This didn't appear to be a robbery gone wrong; the murders were all too personal." Nothing made sense to him. "…and where was Jacob?" It was too much to process. Brian was wrapped up in a horrific mystery he couldn't comprehend and was scared to death.

In the narrow hallway, Brian felt claustrophobic and needed to move. He briefly reflected on his life as he prepared to enter J.J.'s bedroom. Brian recalled the pain of growing up without a mom and his father's years of suffering. He remembered living with his foster parents and the incredible love and compassion that Bishop had shown him. Brian recollected endless hours spent studying the Bible and the pride he felt as he was anointed into the priesthood. He recalled his move to Ashford and the friendships he had formed. The memories washed over Brian like he was experiencing a heavy dose of déjà vu. Everything in his life led him to this moment. He could not turn and run even if he wanted to. There was nowhere else to go but through the door before him.

Unlike Father Jacob, Brian felt no almighty spirit protecting him from evil. On the contrary, he had done nothing but question his faith in God since he had entered the house, and as he turned the doorknob, the doubt grew stronger.

Thoughts of the Bunnyman were the last thing on his mind as he slowly opened the door.

Chapter Eighteen

Father Brian held his hand on the knob as he pushed the door halfway open. The only section of the room he could see was directly before him, where the sun's rays supplied light. The remainder of the room was positioned to his right and blocked from sight. All the blinds were pulled, and the air was stagnant and hot. It smelt heavily of urine and body odor.

Brian opened the door a bit further, relief filling his body as he laid eyes on J.J. The small boy was still sitting on his bed with his legs crossed. He held an Easter basket in his lap and wore Easter Bunny ears on his head. Although Brian wanted to run to J.J., something stopped him from proceeding further into the room. J.J.'s eyes were wide open, and he looked in Brian's direction but did not speak or move.

Brian could not imagine what the poor boy had witnessed. He calmly called to J.J. from behind the safety of the door. "J.J., hey, it's Father Brian. It's safe now, buddy. I've come to get you out of here. Can you walk over to me? I'll take you somewhere safe, I promise."

J.J.'s bunny ears flapped as the boy shook his head back and forth, refusing to do as Brian asked. Still not wanting to enter the room, Brian pleaded with the boy. "I know you're scared, J.J., but we have to get you somewhere safe. Father Jacob is here, too, so let's get out of here…together. Come on, bud, what do you say?"

J.J. closed his eyes and shook his head more forcefully this time. He continued to shake his head and showed no sign of stopping. J.J. was clearly in shock. Brian had no choice but to enter the room and pick him up. Still gripping a knife in his left hand, Brian knew he couldn't carry the child holding the weapon. Reluctantly, he stuck the knife's handle under his belt, blade facing the floor, just ahead of his left hip. Brian was concerned that he may cut himself as they fled, but he was unwilling to give up his weapon.

Swinging the door open to his right, Brian bound toward the child. He stopped beside the bed and reached for the boy's Easter basket. It was a large woven basket, and the handle looped almost above J.J.'s head. Brian grabbed it from J.J.'s lap as he looked at the boy. His first thought was how heavy the basket was. His second thought was the realization that J.J. was sitting in a large puddle of his own urine. Brian examined the basket's contents and, with a gasp, dropped it back into the boy's lap.

Brian backed away from the bed in horror. Michael's head was set inside the basket amongst a layer of pink grass lining. His face stared upward at his younger brother, and the same milky blue haze Brian had seen in Dave's dead eye covered his pupils. Dry blood trails ran from his nostrils and open mouth. J.J. grabbed the long handle on each side of the basket and held it firmly on his lap, continuing to shake his head.

The Simmons house had finally broken him. Brian

felt there was nothing more he could do for the boy; there was no recovery. There was nothing left for Brian to do but run. His mind was prepared to turn and flee, but his body was frozen in fear. Brian felt someone approaching from behind as he willed his body to move. As the figure approached, Brian could see a tall, thin shadow on the wall behind J.J. Just as he was about to reach for his knife; Brian recognized the blue sleeve of the old priest's jacket. Father Jacob stopped silent at Brian's side, and both men stood two feet from the boy. Brian was delirious and had not yet taken his eyes off J.J. He cried out to Jacob, "Where have you been?" He did not wait for an explanation. "Shit, Jacob…look in the basket! We need to get out of here, NOW!" Brian desperately wanted to leave, but he could not get his legs to move.

Brian continued to stare at the boy and his basket without bothering to turn to face Jacob. "Jacob! Michael's head is in that basket, and J.J. won't let go of it. He won't come to me, and I can't carry him alone. Let him hold onto the basket if he wants. We can grab him together, carry him out, and end this. Either way, I am leaving…I don't care. I can't spend one more minute in this house." Brian did not hesitate to ask, "Jacob, say something…will you help me?"

Jacob offered no answer, and the only response Brian received was a weak cough mixed with odd laughter. As Brian turned to face the old priest, he felt the sudden stab of a hundred needles entering his back just below his rib cage. He yelled in shock and pain as he faced his attacker. Brian pushed on the left shoulder of the blue jacket, and the figure stumbled away from him.

Brian had been stabbed. The blade had penetrated his right kidney and sliced into his colon. He spun to the floor, clutching his back where he felt the excruciating pain. The knife was no longer in his back, and warm blood flowed from the gash. Brian pulled his knife from his belt and swung it frantically in front of his body. Falling to his knees, Brian shuffled backward until he reached the wall a few feet behind. He rested his body against it as he inched his way into an upright position, staining the wall red as he stood.

A tall, slender man stood stepped out of the shadows and entered the sunlight, stopping in front of the door. He wore Father Jacob's jacket, but it was not the old priest. He was about the same age as Jacob but completely bald. Brian realized the man had purposely worn Jacob's jacket to catch him off guard. The imposter reached for the door and swung it shut. Brian attempted to yell, "No!" but doubled over in pain.

Brian noticed that J.J. had finally stopped shaking his head. The boy looked towards the man as if waiting for a command. Brian knew Jacob must be in the room and squinted into the darkness. He finally located his friend sitting in the shadows of the room's far corner. Jacob's jacket had been removed, and his body had been propped up. His legs were positioned straight before him, his shoulders slumped, and his arms hung to the floor. Jacob's head was tilted to the side, and his eyes were somewhat open, but he did not blink. A small amount of blood ran from Jacob's nose to his upper lip and mouth. Brian moaned in anguish and began to sob. He did not expect to see a soul leave Jacob's body.

The young priest knew he had entered the seventh circle of hell.

Chapter Nineteen

The man looked at J.J. and smiled. "The boy will not come to you because I have told him not to move. Doesn't he listen well? He's such a good student." He pointed the knife in Jacob's direction. "I cannot take the credit for your friend's demise. His heart took it upon itself to do the work for me." The man's voice was raspy and dry. It sounded old but not frail. "Jacob was shocked when I revealed myself to him...or maybe it was the sight of the boy's head in the basket?" He croaked out a gruff laugh. J.J. followed every step the madman made as he walked a few feet closer to Brian. His knife was still covered in Brian's blood as he held it by his side. Brian was in too much pain to move, so all he could do was brace himself against the wall and wait.

As the man stepped out of the shadows, Brian saw he had a similar build to Jacob, but the face staring down at him was distant and twisted. His soulless eyes, both onset with cataracts, were sunk deep into their sockets and had the milky blue appearance of a dead man. He had no visible eyebrows, and his gray beard was patchy with stubble. Blood spatter covered his face, and his clothing had been permanently stained. He smiled at Brian with a toothless grin.

J.J. turned his head in Brian's direction as the killer spoke again. "Another man of the cloth! What a blessing to have you both join us today...and on such a Holy day!" He released another gravelly laugh.

"I don't believe we have met, young man. On the other hand," he pointed to Jacob's lifeless body, "Father Jacob and I go way back, but it doesn't matter." The man shrugged his shoulders. "I don't even know why I'm mentioning it. I suppose it's because I know my secret is safe here. After all, all secrets are safe in a confessional booth....and now this room appears to be mine."

The man introduced himself. "My name is Thomas Simmons. But there is no need for you to share yours with me. I don't mean to be rude, but your name is irrelevant to me...just as you are irrelevant to me...just as your God and Lord are irrelevant to me." He then scolded Brian. "You have interfered where you are not meant to be. Do you know the family that lived here? Do you have any idea who I am?"

Brian did not break from Thomas's stare as he nodded. He tried to raise his voice but could no longer find the energy. His words came out in a whisper. "Dave, Cindy, and their children were part of my congregation. They were my friends, you sick son of a bitch!" He winced in pain as he spoke. Brian glanced towards the bed and saw J.J.'s attention was upon him. He struggled to push himself off the wall. "J.J. put the basket down! Get up and run!" Brian pointed his knife toward the closed door and then at Thomas.

J.J. showed no emotion as he shuffled on the wet sheets of his bed but did not get up. Instead, he kept the Easter basket on his lap and turned his head quickly towards Thomas, who laughed hysterically. "I told you already, Father, the boy will not move until I tell him. Now answer me! Do you know who I am?"

Brian knew he was dealing with a psychopath. He recalled Jacob telling him Thomas had died, believing he had dementia. Perhaps Brian had misunderstood. Nothing had truth or meaning any longer. All Brian knew was that he was dying. He had to get J.J. out of the house and away from this demon. Brian stumbled back into the wall. Holding his knife with both hands, Brian used his elbows to squeeze his sides, attempting to ease the pain. The room spun, and he dropped down to his right knee. "I know who you are… I know everything. Jacob told me you were dead."

Thomas cackled a hoarse reply. "I'm sure he did. No matter; I thought the same of him. I wondered for a moment if I was staring at a ghost." He slowly shook his head, "He must have felt the same. I could tell he was in shock when he saw my face." Thomas gestured toward Jacob's body as a wry smile spread across his face. "Apparently, I have the stronger heart."

Knowing Brian had no strength left, Thomas pulled a chair from the desk and sat down a few feet away. He wanted to be at eye level with the fallen priest. Thomas asked, "So you have heard of the Bunnyman, Father? You know about my family's legacy?"

Brian whispered, "I know of no legacy, only the work of the devil. Jacob told me about the heroism of your brother, Frank, and his pursuit of your younger brother, John. I know after terrorizing the town in a stolen rabbit costume, he was found hanging from Bunnyman Bridge." Brian took in a shallow breath. The pain in his body had numbed as he slipped into shock. "I also know you were caught under that same bridge, wearing John's mask. I was told about your crimes, and I read the newspaper stories. Jacob told me you had dementia and had been sent to a hospital to be cared for. He had heard little about you...like I said, he thought you were dead."

Thomas was impressed. "So you know of my brother Franklin. He was such a tortured man. I had forgotten that Frank and Jacob were friends, but it's all returning to me now." Thomas clapped his hands. "I thought you fools had ruined my aspirations, but this may even be better than before!" He smiled his toothless grin. "I can only imagine the thoughts running through Jacob's mind when he saw me. I hope some were of Frank's complete failure to destroy our family's legacy. I hope Franklin's suffering never ends, even after death."

Thomas continued his rant. "Frank and Richard wanted me committed. I did not suffer from dementia, you fool," Thomas hissed, "That was an excuse my family used to protect themselves and their precious reputations. They kept me locked away in that god-forsaken hospital. My brothers had the money and the right connections. They wanted me gone, and they got their wish." Thomas mused, "Oh, what I could have done if I hadn't been caught. If only my brothers hadn't turned their backs on me and our family's destiny."

"That is why I am here today...to redeem myself. My brother, Johnny Boy, would not have been pleased with my prior performance." Thomas sounded insane as he explained. "My turn as the Bunnyman ended far too short, and my family took no time making me disappear. I was locked away and forgotten about. They abandoned me for their benefit and precious namesake, and now it is time to take revenge."

"Plenty more needs to be done, but that will not concern you, my new friend. That will be another family affair." Thomas rose from his chair. "Joshua James called his aunts earlier. My nieces are always so willing to help. Sweet, kind Gina and Penny should arrive shortly." Thomas walked to J.J. and cupped the side of his head with his left hand. "The boy gave such a fine performance when he talked with his Aunt Penny. He was a brave young man, making the phone call in front of his parents' corpses. His unsuspecting aunties will bring some cold medicine and perhaps some warm chicken soup. It seems the whole family has come down with a nasty virus. Only little J.J. was well enough to make the phone call."

Thomas laughed as he smiled at the boy. "Aunt Penny was so relieved to hear from him. They had become quite concerned when David's family missed church this morning. I had assumed it was those two witches climbing the steps earlier, but it was just you two fools." Thomas pointed at J.J. as he turned towards Brian. "I will eliminate one of them when they arrive, as planned. One of his aunts must live, though. Someone has to take care of the boy until he is older. But never fear; she will die soon enough."

Brian pleaded with Thomas. "Just let the boy go. You have no way to escape this."

Thomas laughed at the young Priest. "Yes, Father. You are right. I assume the hospital is well aware of my escape, and a search is being conducted. They will find the stolen car soon enough. I know my time is limited…my turn as the Bunnyman will end today. It will end as I had planned…in this house, sitting atop our family's first property. Don't worry one bit; of course, I will let the boy go. I have groomed young Joshua James well. Don't you see? The title will now be passed on to him. I have taught him what he needs to know. You should consider this experience an honor." Thomas pointed his knife first at Brian and then at J.J.

"Behold…the new Bunnyman! "

Chapter Twenty

Thomas further explained his plan. "Young Joshua and I have spent many hours together. Perhaps he has witnessed more than a boy his age should, but it was a necessary step in his training. He has endured the screams of his mother and sister. He has experienced the coldness of his father's dead body and stomached the beheading of his brother. He tolerated watching a man of the cloth die in agony." He looked to J.J. as if lost in a blissful memory. "We had such a wonderful time together." Thomas twirled his knife in his hand. "And yet, there are more memories for Joshua to make!"

He walked over to J.J. and slowly knelt by the boy. "Joshua understands why his family had to die. He knows they never loved him or accepted him for who he was. He knows his parents considered him a mistake. He knew he would never be loved like Michael or Elizabeth. He knows none of them would see things our way. Joshua knows he will be the last Simmons remaining once my nieces die. In the blink of an eye, he will be rich. Joshua can carry on the Bunnyman legacy in any way he chooses. There will be endless resources at his fingertips, enabling him to create misery and terror, cause pain and suffering, enact revenge on his enemies, wreak havoc and fear, and destroy reputations while bolstering the Bunnyman's legacy. He will carry on what his family has created."

Thomas moved closer to Brian and looked him directly in the eyes. "I have relieved this boy of his soul. Look at him, Father. He cares for no one. He has no shame or empathy. He is cold and ruthless. He is the Bunnyman."

Brian shook his head, refusing to listen to the ravings of a lunatic. He did not speak to Thomas but pleaded with J.J., "Joshua, please listen to me. It's Father Brian. I am your mom and dad's friend. They loved you so, so much. Joshua… J.J., this man is crazy. Don't listen to a word he is saying. None of it is true. You must run. I'm begging you…find the power in the Lord."

J.J. still refused to move. There was no sign of emotion or expression on his small face. Thomas stood and walked back to the middle of the room as he mocked Brian. "Find the Lord...I'm afraid he will not be found today. He cannot save you or the boy."

Brian inched his way back up the wall as Thomas spoke. "Let me quote you some lines from the book of your Lord, Father. I feel young Joshua should hear this, even if they do come from such a ridiculous source." He cleared his throat and spoke. "Let the earth fear the LORD; let all people revere him. The LORD foils nations' plans: he thwarts the purposes of the peoples. But the plans of the LORD stand firm forever, the purposes of his heart through all generations."

Thomas smiled and spoke calmly. "You see, pitiful man, this is our family's destiny." He spread his arms like he was hanging on a crucifix. Slouching his shoulders, Thomas dropped his chin to the floor and shouted, "The Bunnyman is the LORD!"

Thomas raised his eyes toward Brian and smiled. "You will be Joshua's final test. If he is successful, your final memory will be that of the new Bunnyman."

Brian felt his life slipping away as he leaned against the wall. He did not want to hear more of the Lord from this false prophet. Brian was not concerned with his own salvation. He only knew there were three lives to save, and that is what he must do.

This nightmare had to end, and Brian had to act now. He would have to commit the ultimate sin; there was no other way. Brian would have to kill this man to save innocent lives, damming his soul to hell. Brian begged the Lord for forgiveness with the bit of faith he had left. Unknowingly, Bishop had sent him on this journey many years earlier. Any hopes of ever seeing his friend again were gone.

Thomas taunted Brian, "You are at peace with death, are you not? After all, you must have a special spot waiting for you in Heaven. Isn't salvation a guarantee for a man of the cloth?" He looked at Brian, expecting an answer.

Brian pushed himself off the wall as Thomas asked his question. Brian let out a wail of anguish and pain, suffering and desperation, sorrow and guilt. Brian cried out for his absent father and forgotten mother, for Bishop and Father Jacob, for Dave, Cindy, and their children. He found strength when he thought he had nothing left. Brian lunged at the psychopath, catching him off-guard. Brian pushed his blade into Thomas' side and buried it deep into his lung. After he felt the knife go into Thomas' flesh, Brian immediately dropped to his knees.

Thomas let go of his knife and fell to his knees, as well. He could no longer talk as blood had started to fill his lungs. He looked at Brian with hatred in his dead eyes and motioned towards J.J. Brian felt dizzy, and his vision was blurred. However, he saw Joshua set his basket down and make his way to Thomas. Brian's eyes began to close as he watched Thomas pull J.J. toward him and whisper in his ear. J.J. listened intently to his fallen mentor and then removed his bunny ears. He placed them on Thomas's bald head. The boy then pulled on the knife handle embedded into Thomas' torso. J.J. removed it and placed it in Thomas' hands.

Brian fell flat to the floor, closed his eyes, and braced himself for his final moments of pain and suffering, but they didn't come. Instead, Brian heard an awful gurgling sound. He was able to crack his eyes open just enough to see Thomas slicing his own throat. The Bunnyman held an appalling grin on his face until death overtook him. His pale eyes rolled into his skull, and he hit the floor.

J.J. now stood between the grown men; one was dead, and one was dying. He reached for Thomas, grabbed the bunny ears off his head, and placed them back onto his own. Brian looked up at J.J., unable to move. The bedroom carpet felt soft on his cheek as his eyes closed. J.J. spoke for the first time.

"Great-Uncle Thomas is dead now. It is time to go, Father Brian."

Chapter Twenty-One

Traffic was heavier than expected. Carol and Sam Holt arrived at her sister's house in Fishersville later than they had hoped. The couple was rushed into the Easter celebration at the house, and Carol had forgotten her worries back home. It wasn't until a few hours later that she remembered the Simmons' odd absence from church and made the call to St. Mary's. When they told her the priests had never arrived, the couple prepared to return home. Just as they were about to leave, they saw a breaking news bulletin on the local T.V. station. Their road had been closed, and a S.W.A.T. team was in place. With deep concern, they decided to stay with Carol's sister to avoid the chaos.

Gina and Penny drove into their cousin Dave's driveway as the sun descended toward the horizon. The thirsty earth had soaked up most of the flood waters, and the scent of spring was fresh in the air. Suddenly, J.J. ran from the front door in hysterics. As he raced to the car, his bunny ears flew off. He was covered in blood and smelled of urine. J.J. repeated, "They're all dead," over and over. The two sisters were convinced their nephew spoke the truth after seeing their niece in the church's sedan.

Gina stripped J.J. of his soiled clothes and wrapped him in a blanket from her car. They placed him onto the back seat and made the short drive to the Holts.

Penny broke through a small window on the back door and retrieved their phone. Fortunately, the lines had been repaired, and they could call for help. The police and paramedics arrived shortly after.

What the police found was a true house of horrors, a walk through hell. They relived the nightmare that Jacob and Brian had unknowingly walked into. The police found the entire family, just as the two priests had. Elizabeth was found lying in the sedan's backseat, her legs broken and throat slit. Dave was on his bed with a perfectly placed knife in one eye. Cindy lay on the bedroom floor with a knife protruding out of her hand. Michael's mutilated body was in the bathtub, and his head was in his brother's room. Father Jacob was also found in J.J.'s bedroom propped up in the corner. They found Thomas Simmons, the escaped patient from the psychiatric hospital, in the same room with his throat slit.

Not far from Thomas's corpse, Brian lay on his stomach with his eyes closed. His head was turned to the side, resting on the carpet where he had watched J.J. place the bunny ears on his head. Thomas' knife had been shoved deep into Brian's left ear. The blade stood at attention, straight into the air and straight to Heaven.

J.J. knew he would have to be patient. His time would come. He watched the house fade out of sight through the back window of the ambulance as they drove away from his family's home. Aunt Penny sat next to him, holding his hand. J.J. knew his aunts would take good care of him; he was sure of it. If the two priests hadn't interfered with Uncle Thomas' plan, there would only be one of them left, but it didn't really matter. They were growing old and would be dead soon enough. One day, they would be gone, and then he could begin. He needed them now.

After all, he was just a boy, but someday he would be the Bunnyman.

About the Author

162

Joel Hayes was born in 1976 in Wisconsin and has lived within the state his entire life. He currently resides in Fond du Lac with his wife, Dawn and has two children, Zoe and Max. This is his first novel.